C000297432

S. Aslam was born and raised in South Yorkshire. He has worked in the clinical research sector for over seventeen years, helping to bring medicines onto the market to help improve the lives of people.

This book is dedicated to the best boxer of all time Muhammad Ali (1942-2016) and all of his fans.

"May Allah (s.w.t) bless you with the highest ranks in Jannah (heaven)."

S. Aslam

THE BUTTERFLY WILL ALWAYS FLOAT

AUSTIN MACAULEY PUBLISHERS™

LONDON • CAMBRIDGE • NEW YORK • SHARJAH

A CIP catalogue record for this title is available from the British Library.

ISBN 9781528936019 (Paperback)
ISBN 9781528989961 (Hardback)
ISBN 9781528989978 (ePub e-book)

www.austinmacauley.com

First Published 2021
Austin Macauley Publishers Ltd®
1 Canada Square
Canary Wharf
London
E14 5AA

Thank you Muhammad Ali for being 'The Greatest' boxer of all time inside and outside of the ring.

1. <u>EXT. MANGAL'S BOXING GYM. SHANTY
   TOWN. MUMBAI</u> 1

It's a wet and windy night in the city of Mumbai. Away from
all the glitz and glamour in the commercial capital is a hellish
life on the streets, begging, cringing, with no self-respect. The
Mumbai of the hard-working poor. The Mumbai of the
aspiring migrant, with his fierce drive for survival, for self-
improvement. The Mumbai of small enterprise. The Mumbai
of cottage industries. The Mumbai of poor yet strong women,
running entire households on the strength of their income
from collecting and selling rubbish, working as labourers,
maids and cleaners. Every morning, these women put food on
the table, braid their daughters' hair and send them to either
work or schools. They have hope for the future; this is the
Mumbai of dreams. Almost half of its 12 million people live
in slums or dilapidated buildings. They are located on open
land, along railway tracks, on pavements, next to the airport,
under bridges and along the city's coastline. One such
shantytown is Kaali Basti (Black shantytown), named so
because of its illicit drug peddling. Two hundred families live
in the most abominable conditions. Packed like sardines in a
tin box, they are holed up in small ramshackle houses without
any basic amenities. They have to share one public toilet and

one bathroom, which are without proper doors. The only way one knows if the total is occupied is by singing loudly whilst using. In this deprived locality, like most across the world, drugs, crime and prostitution is the order of the day in this and surrounding *bastis*. On the main lane towards the bazaar, there is an old gym on the corner with an old signboard reading 'Warriors Gym.' As you walk into the gym, there is a poster of Amjad Khan a.k.a Gabbar Singh (an iconic villain character in Hindi cinema) with the caption '*Ab tera kya hoga kaalia*' (now what's going to happen to you darky)? And close by, there is another notice reading 'WARNING: Children left unattended will be sold.' To the left, you have a locker room with a shower and a sign reading. 'Enter at own risk.' Then on the right, you have a small notice board with nothing but an advertisement for an upcoming amateur boxing tournament and straight ahead a huge hall with a blue boxing ring in the middle with two prospects sparring in the middle of the ring and a would-be promoter watching on for a future champion that will earn him his bread. On the heavy bag, you have a middle-aged pummelling the bag like his mistress and other unsavoury thugs like characters scattered around the gym.

As soon as you walk into the gym, you can feel it. It's a boxing atmosphere. There are people on the side lines, and everybody's got their own opinion of you, and nobody's scared to say anything—everybody speaks their mind. People from all walks of life

We see a young *Jaan* (English meaning soul, life), a.k.a Johnny (a 12-year-old overweight boy being brought up by a single mother) sweeping the floor. As he is sweeping the floor, he looks up at a poster of Boxer Muhammad Ali (previously known as Cassius Clay).

Mangal
(a.k.a. Two Teeth)
A 72-year-old man, ex-boxer, was a promising amateur and tipped to become a world champion. But war intervened, cutting his career short. That robbed him of his best years and he ended up in a black-hole of obscurity like most of that era.

"Hey, Johnny boy, you cleaned out Goofy's locker?"
Johnny nods his head to say yes.

Mangal
"You better get going as you got school in the morning."

Just coming into view and taking the sweeping brush from Johnny.

Mangal
"Gimme that and get going."

On his way into the town many years ago, Mangal saw Johnny being bullied and helped him and, ever since then, had taken him under his wing. Mangal has never had children of his own as his wife died of small pox soon after Mangal returned from war. But if he had children, his grandson would have been the age of Johnny. Johnny helps around the gym after school, and in return, Mangal lets him watch one video recording of a Muhammad Ali fight per week from his archive every Friday. For Johnny, the best day of his week.

Johnny heads for the exit. As he walks across the gym hall, he looks around at the life-sized poster of Muhammad Ali and looks down at the words on the poster that reads float like a butterfly.

2 EXT. A LANE OF SHANTY HUTS IN A
   DEPRIVED AREA OF MUMBAI. 2

A sprawl of predominately small huts in a *basti* (slum) with a huge skyscraper in the distance at the end of a derelict section of houses. The area is cheap, with abandoned cars and bags of rubbish scattered around, giving an impression that no one cares about this place. Drugs, anti-social behaviour, crime and corruption seem to be the order of the day.

3 INT. INSIDE JOHHNYS HOUSE. MUMBAI. 3

Johnny walks into the house and trips over some needles. He shares this derelict house with many other families from the slum who have squatted here for many years. He has his own little room (*kholi*) that he shares with his mother.

He uses the steps and walks all the way up to the last floor. As he gets to the floor, he is sweating and can barely lift his school bag. Johnny walks around the corner towards the room and finds a muscular man shouting and threatening his mum.

<u>Man</u>
"I want that money by next week, you bitch, or you're going to be out on the street."

The man walks out of the flat as Johnny walks towards him through a haze of spliff smoke (marijuana leaves rolled into a cigarette for smoking).

Man

(to Johnny)

"Out of my way, you fat fuck."

4 INT. KITCHEN. INSIDE KHOLI. MUMBAI. 4

Johnny walks into the place and sees his mum snorting some cocaine on a crate which is the make-do kitchen table.

Mum

(whilst sniffling her nose)

"Did you get paid today?"

Johnny takes a note out of his pocket that his mum snatches out of his hand as she grabs her coat.

Mum

"I'm off."

Mum makes her way out and turns back

Mum

"Have you been eating junk food again?"

Johnny nods his head to say no.

Mum

(angrily)

"You have, haven't you?"

Johnny nods his head to say no.

Mum

(whilst grabbing his stomach)

"Look at you. You fucking embarrass me. My friends are always taking the piss out of you. Why do you have to show me up? Can't you be fucking normal like other kids? Why do you have to be so fat?"

Mum slaps Johnny across the head and Johnny begins to cry.

Mum

"I haven't got time for this. You're about as useful as a pair of sunglasses on a bloke with one ear."

Mum puts her jacket on. Take a cigarette box out of her pocket and lights a cigarette.

Mum

"I'm off."

She comes back to the crate and snorts the remaining spots of cocaine, then walks off, slamming the door behind her, which is falling apart anyway.

Johnny wipes his tears and goes to one of the cupboards in the kitchen and tries to reach for something at the back of the cupboard without any success. So he drags the crate across, which is the make-do kitchen table across the floor and stands on it to take at a small bag from behind all the boxes. He opens it up to find two soggy doughnuts, one of which he drops accidentally treads on but picks it up, dusting off any dirt and then eats both doughnuts with pleasure.

Johnny then walks into the corner part of the *kholi*, his make-do bedroom that is small, compact and full of boxes, but on the walls, there are many posters of Muhammad Ali, whom he idolises. He lies down on his bed, where he falls asleep until the next morning.

One of the posters on the wall is of Indian Screen legend Amitabh Bachan (Famous Bollywood Actor of Hindi cinema) with the words. Everyone wants to be like AB written on the bottom. Then next to this, in a 12-year-old's handwriting, Johnny has written: "Not me. I want to be like Ali."

5   EXT. ST THOMAS SCHOOL MUMBAI. 5

We see a busy Mumbai street full of school morning traffic. The noise of passing taxis, shouting and swearing; groups of children congregating at the huge iron gates that inaugurate the entrance to the old Victorian buildings that look more like a factory than a school. The elder children make their way around the corner for a quick cigarette before duty calls. St Thomas School, once one of the most prestigious schools in the region now rated one of the worst in Mumbai. The school accommodates children from the ages 11-16, all from very poor and violent backgrounds, a haven for local drug dealers and pimps. St Thomas was established in the 1950s for rich families to send their upper-class rich posh kids. In other words, it was for kids with a silver spoon stuck up their ass. Over the years, it's become a free for all. Just over 900 students walk through these gates every day.

Eleven of these students will pass their exams and go onto college, which is just over 1%. Just 1% of the school population making use of an education that is free to everybody. You're probably thinking about what happens to all the other poor souls.

About 100 of the students will drop out before they reach the final year because they have to work and support the family as they can't afford to carry on with their schooling as the main breadwinner in their family falls into one of the following categories:

A. Someone who has excessive consumption of alcohol and can't hold a job down for more than a few days and needs help = Alcoholic
B. Someone who has excessive consumption of drugs and can't hold a job down for more than a few days and needs help = Druggie or Junky
C. Someone who is hardworking, takes responsibility for his family, pays taxes and works all the hours he/she can, but it's still not enough = Normal People
D. Someone who just sits at home all day watching cricket and drinking alcohol while the wife is struggling at work and looking after the kids = Loser

About 1.6% of the female student population will fall pregnant and will drop out as a result. That's 15 girls dropping out of school because they took the sexual education part of the curriculum too literally.

Around seven students will start experimenting with drugs. Normally in the second year. They will be attracted to the high life and will be head-hunted by a local drug dealer or *bhai* who will get them to do the errands and dirty work. By the age of 14 or 15, most of them will earn as much as their fathers, who spend most of their time slaving away for next to nothing. These kids will have flashy clothes and financial income, attracting another seven kids to the same line of work, then that will attract another seven. It's like the domino effect. In the end, you will have ten times more than what you started with. That's 70 kids, 7.7% of the school population, who instead of being the next bunch of doctors, engineers and teachers become drug users, dealers and criminals. Instead of improving society, they are abusing society. That's not only 70 kids but that's also 70 families, maybe 70 mothers, maybe 70 fathers, brothers, sisters. That's 70 families destroyed.

The ones who have ambition and can take care of themselves will go and find work that isn't many of them.

Five hundred of the students, over 50%, will go through the motions and complete school then end up in dead-end jobs, some doing better than others. About 30 will be so frustrated and angry at the system that they will take the law into their own hands, ending up in prison.

The remaining 17% (154 students) will fall into the categories mentioned earlier: Alcoholic, Junkie, or Loser. It's a vicious cycle that goes round and round. The truth is God helps those who help themselves and until that change comes, the cycle will continue to go round and round, especially in a place like Kaali Basti.

6   INT. CORRIDOR. ST THOMAS SCHOOL.
     MUMBAI. 6

September: first day back after the summer holidays.

We can hear noise from inside the classroom, kids screaming and laughing and a teacher shouting to maintain order.

Just coming into view is Johnny (12 yrs.), with his huge legs and fat body walking down the corridor steadily. Then a group of older kids (15 yr. olds) run down the corridor after him.

Kid 1 (a.k.a Shorty)
(to Johnny)
Hey, look who it is?

Kid 2 (a.k.a Slick)
(to Shorty)
Look at his trainers. He's
such a tramp.

Kid 3 (a.k.a Big Brother)
(to Shorty & Slick)
He's so fat.

Kid 1 (a.k.a Shorty)
(to Johnny)
He's so fat when you went
to school, you sat next to
everybody.

Kid 2 (a.k.a Slick)
(to Shorty)
I wouldn't say he's fat but
he has more chins than a Hong
Kong telephone directory.

Kid 2 (a.k.a Slick)
(to Johnny)
You could be in the movies—
you could play crowd scenes
all by yourself.

Kid 1 (a.k.a Shorty)
(to Johnny)
Is it alright if I sell you're
underwear to the circus? I hear
they need a new tent.

Kid 2 (a.k.a Slick)
(to Johnny)
Is that your stomach, or did you
swallow a beach ball?

Kid 1 (a.k.a Shorty)
(to Johnny)
What about his mamma? Your
mamma so fat I took a picture
of her last Christmas/Diwali
and it's still printing.

                    Teacher
                    (to all)
               Hey, what's going on?

               Kid 1 (a.k.a Shorty)
                   (to Teacher)
             Nothing Sir. We're just going
                 to our next class.

                    Teacher
                    (to all)
             Well, don't just stand there.
                 Get a move on.

             Kid 3 (a.k.a Big Brother)
               (whispers to Johnny)
           You're mamma so fat she puts on her
               lipstick with a paint roller.

The kids laugh apart from Johnny, who is frightened

7   INT. BOYS TOILET. ST THOMAS SCHOOL.
     MUMBAI. 7

    Johnny goes into the toilet and goes to the cubicle, puts
the toilet seat down and closes the cubicle door, sitting there
in a state. Moments later, he hears the door open and footsteps
walking towards the cubicle and then to the sink. He hears
someone wash their hands, use the dryer and the door opens
and shuts. He opens the cubicle door to have a look, and as he
does, Shorty and Slick grab him and push him into the toilet

cubicle. Big Brother walks into the cubicle as Shorty steps out to keep a look out for anyone coming into the toilet. Johnny is pleading and crying, asking them to let him go in the name of God, saying he has no other clothes to wear, but his pleading falls on deaf ears as Big Brother, who is much bigger and older than Johnny, holds his head with force and pushes it towards the toilet as Slick flushes it. They all laugh, making fun of Johnny, and run out of the cubicle and the toilets, leaving Johnny soaked and crying.

Johnny gets back to his feet and makes his way to the sink whilst sobbing. He washes his face and his mouth out, spitting out the horrible taste of toilet water and washes it out with tap water. He places his wet-shirt under the dryer in an attempt to dry off the toilet water.

As he is drying his shirt, one of the teachers walks into the toilets.

Teacher

(to Johnny)

Why aren't you in your

class?

Before Johnny can answer, the teacher sees the mess in the toilets and assumes Johnny is the culprit or more due to the fact Big Brother is the son of the local goon, so he wouldn't get the blame.

Teacher

(shouting at Johnny)

What the hell have you been

doing here?

Without giving Johnny a chance to explain, the teacher drags Johnny by the collar out of the toilet and to the headmaster's office.

Moments later, Johnny comes back into the toilet to get his bag. As he is doing so, he takes a few tissues and tries to wipe some of the water off his shorts as it looks like he has wet himself. At that point, the teacher rushes back into the toilet and grabs Johnny taking him off his feet, dragging him away.

Teacher

(angrily to Johnny)

It's a bit late for that now.

You should have thought of

that before.

8   INT.HEADMASTERS OFFICE. ST THOMAS SCHOOL. MUMBAI. 8

The teacher explains to the headmaster why Johnny has been summoned, after which Johnny is told that he will be kept in detention for the rest of the week for making a mess in the toilet. The headmaster slaps Johnny around the head whilst cursing him again and again.

Johnny looks over at the time on the clock that slowly moves on.

9   EXT. SCHOOL GATES. ST THOMAS SCHOOL. MUMBAI. 9

Johnny makes his way out of school when someone shouts at him from behind.

Girl

(shouts at Johnny)

Hey you!

Johnny looks around, and a group of boys (including Shorty and Slick) and girls shouting his name, poking fun at him, start to run after Johnny. Johnny begins to run, and even though he has a head start, his excessive weight doesn't allow him to get very far, and the others catch up with him.

One of the girls pushes Johnny whilst one of the boys kneels down behind him, making him fall to the ground. Once again, Johnny is humiliated as the boys and girls turn away as the bus arrives just outside the school. Johnny stands up and begins to pick up his books that were taken out of his bag and thrown all over the grass just outside the school. As he is doing so, a boy much younger than Johnny wearing glasses with goofy teeth, carrying a very heavy bag walks over, puts his own bag down and helps Johnny pick up his books. Johnny is overwhelmed, as he's never had anyone give him a helping hand. Johnny wipes his tears, and they both retrieve all his books and put them back in his bag. Johnny acknowledges the other boy who walks off before Johnny can say anything to him. Johnny stands there, watching the other guy struggling to carry his heavy bag, so Johnny runs over to help him carry it. This time it's the other boy who is overwhelmed, as he's never had anyone help him before. They both acknowledge each other and walk together, carrying the heavy bag in complete silence.

EXT. MANGALS BOXING GYM. SHANTY TOWN. MUMBAI

Johnny walks into the gym, and as he walks in, he sees a poster for the under 16s annual boxing competition on the notice board. The competition which Big Brother has won for the last three years. As Johnny is staring and trying to read the advert, Mangal comes up behind him.

Mangal

(to Johnny)

Did you forget to turn off

the lights on your way out

last night?

Johnny nods his head to say "no."

Mangal

It must have been a ghost.

Well, those buckets aren't

going to empty themselves.

Johnny nods his head and turns to the changing rooms where he puts his school bag in the locker and starts emptying out the buckets of dirty water from the main hall of the gym into the toilets.

It's now 8:30 pm, and Mangal comes into view.

Mangal

(whilst coughing)

I'm off upstairs, kiddo;

it's the Mike Tyson
fight tonight. Mike's
going to batter that guy
tonight. Make sure you
don't forget to turn the
lights off.

Jimmy nods his head to say "yes."

Mangal makes his way up the stairs at the back of the gym that lead into his small flat at the top of the gym hall.

Johnny finishes stacking up the gloves and looks over at the ring. Then looks over at the poster of Muhammad Ali and makes his way to the ring. Johnny climbs into the ring and falls over. He picks himself up and walks over to the corner of the ring, where he picks up a skipping rope and begins to fold it. Johnny climbs down from the ring and throws the skipping rope into a box with all the others. He steadily walks to the changing rooms past the poster of Muhammad Ali, which falls off the wall. Johnny turns back and tries to stick it back on the wall, but he isn't tall enough, so he walks to the other side of the gym to get a chair. He picks up the chair and brings it near to the wall and stands on it to stick the poster back in its original place on the wall. He steps down from the chair and does the Ali shuffle. As Johnny makes his way to the changing rooms, he feels a breeze, but as he turns around, there's nothing there, and all the windows and doors are closed. Johnny walks into the changing room, picks up his bag and puts on his coat making his way out of the changing room turning the light off. He walks out and turns off the main light for the main hall of the gym, then walks towards the exit. He opens the door and hears a noise; Johnny turns back. He walks back and looks in the changing room and he sees nothing. He can hear someone around the ring area in the main hall.

Johnny is very frightened but plucks up the courage to turn the light on. He turns on the light, and right before his very own eyes, to his amazement, he sees a muscular, tall black man wearing white shorts dancing around in the ring punching the air whilst dancing clockwise and then doing a shuffle.

Johnny looks at the man in the ring then looks at the poster of Muhammad Ali, and the two of them are identical.

Johnny drops his bag and runs into the changing room with his heart beating like a train. He washes his face in the sink, then moments later, peers around the corner from the changing room into the main hall and sees there's nobody in the ring. Thinking he has dreamt this, he walks back to pick up his bag and re-affirms that there's no one in the ring. He picks up his bag and begins again looking around to see if anyone's there, and there's nobody. He walks towards the exit and hears someone muttering the words: "I'm a baaaad man."

Johnny looks around and sees once again, to his amazement, Muhammad Ali shadowboxing in front of the large mirrors that cover the far wall.

<u>Muhammad Ali</u>
(whilst shadowboxing and looking in the mirror)
I'm so pretty, look at me.
I'm so beautiful. I'm the
fastest thing on two feet,
I'm the king of the world,
I am the greatest; I shook up
the world, I am the greatest,

> I'm the king of the world, I'm
> pretty, I'm pretty, I'm
> a bad man, you heard me I'm
> a bad man. I'm the king of the
> world.

Ali does a quick succession of hooks and uppercuts in a matter of seconds. Johnny drops his bag and is hooked. He walks up behind Ali like a zombie and is standing directly behind him. He is mesmerised and in ore of Ali.

<u>Muhammad Ali</u>
(to himself)
Float like a butterfly, sting
like a bee, his hands can't
hit what his eyes can't see.

Ali then looks around at Johnny and smiles.

<u>Johnny</u>
(to Ali in a stuttering voice)
M…m…mmmm…muha…Muhamm…
Mmmuhamm, is that you?

<u>Muhammad Ali</u>
(to Johnny)
You ain't as dumb as you
look, kid.

Then the speedball in the corner of the gym catches Ali's eye and his eyes light up, like a kid entering a candy store. Ali walks past Johnny rubbing his head. Not knowing what is happening and filled with confusion and excitement at the same time, Johnny faints.

Johnny wakes up to find Mangal standing over him, slapping his cheeks.

Mangal
(in a concerned voice)
Wake up, kiddo, wake up.

Johnny sits up on the floor.

Mangal
(to Johnny)
What happened?

Johnny shrugs his shoulders. Then Mangal takes a cup of water and makes Johnny drink it.

Mangal
(to Johnny)
Here drink this.

Mangal asks again.

Mangal
(to Johnny)
What happened, kiddo?

Johnny shrugs his shoulders to say that he doesn't know.

Mangal

(to Johnny)

Did you have anything to eat

today?

Johnny looks over at Mangal in a confused way, as he still hasn't come to terms with what he saw.

Mangal

That's probably it. You need

to get some food down you.

Johnny gets up to his feet and looks over at the clock and the clock shows only ten minutes have passed since he folded up the skipping rope, which leads him to believe he was only dreaming, *but how can that be*, he thinks to himself.

Mangal

(to Johnny)

Get a move on. I've got some

soup upstairs. So let's get

that down you as you need all

the energy you can get. You're

not a flyweight, after all.

You'd be in the super super

heavyweight category if there

was one. (referring to his weight).

Mangal hurriedly makes his way to the stairs at the back of the gym with a slight hobble as Johnny follows him. He walks up the steps.

29

Mangal

(to himself)

I hope Tyson hasn't knocked that

Clown out yet.

They get up to the flat, and Mangal hurries to the TV and is relieved to see the Big Fight Live has gone into a commercial break. He goes into the little kitchen at the corner of the room, takes a saucepan and pours some soup into a bowl.

Johnny is taken aback by the boxing memorabilia Mangal has collected over the years, including pictures of some of the boxing greats: Sugar Ray Robinson, Joe Louis, Rocky Marciano, Muhammad Ali, Sonny Liston, etc. Pair of old boxing gloves catch Johnny's attention.

Mangal walks over to Johnny.

Mangal

(to Johnny whilst handing over a bowl of soup)

Here have this. Got no spoons as

those things are for women. So

drink up.

Mangal sees Johnny looking at the gloves.

Mangal

(to Johnny)

Those gloves were the ones

worn by Rocky Marciano on

October 26th, 1951 when he

fought Joe Louis at the Garden.

It was a sad night, the end
of Louis. One of the great
boxers of our time made to
look ordinary. Not surprisingly,
at 37, he was carrying more
weight than he did in his
prime, and he didn't seem to
carry it well. A bit like you.

Mangal looks over at Johnny.

Mangal
(to Johnny)
He looked significantly smaller
but much more muscular. I do
remember that right from the
opening bell; Marciano started
coming forward, throwing punches
from all angles and that Louis
was in retreat.

Mangal all excited at this stage and demonstrating to
Johnny how the punches were thrown as he drinks his soup
and listens carefully to what Mangal is telling him.

Mangal
(to Johnny)
Sticking his left out in an
attempt to keep the younger
fighter off him. I remember
that Joe Louis was still Joe

31

Louis, and for the first three
or four rounds, he was able to
keep the fight in the middle
of the ring, providing him
with the room to manoeuvre and
avoid Marciano's wild charges
and punches.
Marciano fought every fight
as if it was a street fight
and his strategy was to land
as many punches as often as
possible anywhere on the guy
in front of him. As the fight
progressed, Louis, tiring from
his early mid-ring movement,
began to spend more time on
the ropes and increasingly
became the stationary target
that Marciano was looking for.
The end came in the eighth round;
Louis, back to the ropes and
to the TV camera, caught a
fearsome left hook from Marciano
followed by an overhand right
that sent Louis through the
ropes and out onto the apron
of the ring. I remember it was
clear, on the TV screen, that
sportswriters and maybe
even one of the judges kept
Louis from tumbling off

the apron and into the crowd.
And the thing I remember most
clearly, the thing I have never
forgotten about that night which
is now more than fifty years ago,
is that as everyone watched Joe
Louis cascade through those
ropes and out onto the ring
apron, there wasn't a sound.
All night, fight fans, like my
dad had been shouting at the TV
and now, with the black and white
screen showing Joe Louis sprawled
awkwardly outside the ring in
Madison Square Garden, there was
an eerie sound of silence;
absolute, complete, silence,
the kind of silence you got
at the Church on Sunday, during
Mass, or in a Mosque during prayer.

Then suddenly, in the background, the Big Fight has returned after the commercial break, and Mangal goes and sits in front of the 14-inch television that has a fuzzy picture. Johnny walks over to a crate near the TV and sits there watching the fight until they go into another commercial break

During the commercial break, Johnny asks Mangal.

<u>Johnny</u>
(to Mangal in a stuttering voice)

W…w…what hhhhapppened to Jjjjoo?

Mangal
He fought on too long, kiddo. Owed
a lot of money and died.

Johnny
(to Mangal in a stuttering voice)
Aaaand tttthe rocky guy?

Mangal
He was the only heavyweight boxer
to remain undefeated in history.

Johnny
W…w…what happened to him?

Mangal
He died too. We all gotta die
sometime, kid.

Mangal and Johnny watch the fight end, as Tyson knocks out his opponent in the second round, much to Mangal's disappointment as he just loves boxing and could watch for hours.

Johnny can see how much Mangal loves boxing and asks.

Johnny
(to Mangal in a stuttering voice)
Can I ask you something?

Mangal

Well, spit it out, kiddo.

Johnny

How come you love boxing
so much?

Mangal

Why do I love boxing?

Mangal walks over to the corner of his cabin, where he has some boxing photos and memorabilia. He looks at a picture of Muhammad Ali knocking out George Foreman in 1974 in the Rumble in the Jungle.

Mangal

Why do I love boxing?
Most people see boxing,
not as a sport, but as two
brutes in a ring trying to
hurt each other. They
think I must like boxing
because of the blood and
because the combat
brings me to that primitive
place in my soul. When
you see those guys downstairs
when they are sparring and
they say, "Oh, hit me, please.
It makes me feel like a man."
They are under the wrong

assumption that only
hitting someone and getting
hit will verify that they
are real men. They couldn't
be more wrong. The truth of
the matter is—I love
boxing, but for all the right
reasons. Boxing is the closest
that any sport comes to
purity. It is the sport
that all others aspire to.
It's a reflection of life.
It has all the nasty things
we experience in life like
greed and hate, dishonesty
and corruption, pain and
failure. But it also has
all the good that life has
to offer: pride and grace,
honour and nobility, honesty
and pure pleasure. No other
sport can come close to making
this claim. Why do I love
boxing? I love boxing because
of the self-disciple. Boxing
is a sport of constant training
of both the body and mind.
If you miss a workout, it
will show in the ring.
If you skip your roadwork, it
will show in the ring. If you

skip your spend your time drinking and
carousing, it will show in the
ring. It is a sport of
dedication. A sport where
you can't cut corners, or you
will fail.
Unlike team sports, where
if you slack off a little
a team member can help
you out, in boxing there
is no one else to depend
but yourself. Your
corner can give you
instructions, but you have
to execute them. Your
manager can set up fights,
but you have to win them.
A fighter can be in perfect
shape. His skills can be
sharp as a razor, his
reflexes can be honed like
a jungle cat, but if his
mind is not strong, his body
will fail. In no other
sport is mental strength
so important. You have
the build-up to the
fight, the press conferences
and the weigh-in. During
these times, the fighter
works to intimidate his foe.

The battle has already begun
and the bell for round one
has not even rung. On the
day of the fight is the
walk-ins and the introductions,
but the true test of mental
toughness comes when the
two fighters have to step
up to one another in the
centre of the ring. While
the referee gives the
instructions, the two
combatants stare at each other
down, looking for any sign
of weakness. How many fights
have been won during the stare
down?
Why do I love boxing? I love
boxing because of the
unpredictability. In no
other sport can a person or
team be losing badly and
then, a second later, be
victorious. In football, if
a team is losing by three goals, they need four
goals to win. In boxing,
if a man is losing by nine
rounds, he needs only one
punch, a knockout, to win.
The old saying "You won the
the battle, but I'll win the war,"

has never been truer than in the boxing ring. How can I explain the excitement of watching a fighter who is losing badly on the scorecard deliver one punch to the sweet spot to end the fight? What other sport can deliver that kind of drama?

Why do I love boxing? I love boxing because of the feeling and rush it gives you. Is there any greater feeling in the world than to step between the ropes and into the ring? You feel the lights on your face and your ears buzz from the reaction of the crowd. You stomach twists in fear and you feel nervous energy as you get ready for combat. You look across the ring to see the only person that stands between you and victory. You have to test your strength against that person. You must test his skills, his intelligence and his endurance. You have to test his heart. Do you want it more and have you trained enough to get it? Your only salvation is one minute after every round. Can a person ever feel more alive than when they are in the ring? Is there any joy greater than the taste of victory? Is there anything more bitter then defeat?

Why do I love boxing? I love boxing because of the struggle to be the best. Many casual fans of the sport only enjoy the fights when there is a lot of give and take. If they don't see knockdowns, they feel as if they didn't get their money's worth. But to me, it is everything that comes before the punch. It's the skill and coordination. It's the focus and stamina. It's the footwork that puts the fighter into position to deliver a combination or cut off the ring. Or the way a fighter feints and moves out

of trouble. It's seeing a
fighter against the ropes
ducking punches while moving
only inches to get out of the
way. The slips, bumps and
pushes, the distance, range
and crowding of the boxers
is like a dance. It's poetry
in motion. It is art at its
highest form. It's the sweet
science. It's watching two
professionals with a true
understanding of the trade
putting on a show.

Why do I love boxing? As
important as skills and
understanding of the
profession are to a
fighter, you can never
underestimate heart and
desire. Boxing is about
giving everything you
have despite the
consequences. It's about
determination, durability
and power. It's about
reaching deep inside
yourself and finding out
what type of person you
really are. A person can
never really know what

type of person they are
until they have been
tested and boxing provides
that test. In the ring,
when things are going
badly, is when you really
discover who you are and
what you are about.
Fighters are the most
special of people. They
understand that it's there
job to get into a ring
and fight another person,
but they also understand
that it's a time of self-discovery.
Why do I love boxing? I
love boxing most of all
because boxing, like life,
is an individual sport.
A person goes through life
with the support of
friends and family,
sponsors and their career,
but ultimately, it is up
to the individual to fail
or succeed. The same is
true of the boxer. A fighter
has a trainer to teach him
how to move, punch and
fight. He has a manager
to get him fights and

advance his career. He
has a promoter to expose
him to the public so that
he can make money. But it
is the job of the fighter
to put his fears aside,
step into the ring,
and prove himself. Talent,
skills, luck and knowing
the right people are great,
but heart and passion
are essential to succeeding
in life, as well as in the
ring. Life is an individual
sport and no other sport
mirrors life quite like boxing.
And that's why I love boxing.

Johnny is just mesmerized by Mangal's boxing
knowledge and sits there attentively.

Mangal
Well, go on, kiddo. You
got school in the morning
so get going.

Johnny gets up to leave as Mangal reminds him to turn the
lights off whilst cursing the TV and Don King (a famous
American Boxing promoter with a bad reputation).

Johnny walks down the steps and walks past the ring to
pick up his bag. He walks towards and climbs back into the

ring, and to his amazement, he finds a skipping rope. Earlier, Johnny recalls folding up the same skipping rope and throwing it into the box, after which no one has been in the gym other than Johnny and Mangal. And Mangal wasn't one to skip as he had difficulty walking, never mind skipping.

Johnny is confused, so he leaves the skipping rope in the ring, picks up his bag and walks past the poster of Muhammad Ali. He looks around, hoping Ali will appear but not this time. Johnny makes his way out and turns the lights off.

11 <u>EXT. SCHOOL GATES. ST THOMAS SCHOOL.MUMBAI</u> 11

Johnny turns up at school the next morning, trying to track down the kid who helped him with his books previously, but there is no sign of him. Johnny goes to his class, avoiding the bullies in fear of being beaten up again. He sees Big Brother, Shorty and Slick coming into school and hides behind the door avoiding their attention. The boy he is looking for comes and stands behind him, without Johnny's knowledge. Moments later, Johnny looks around and gets a shock.

The boy uses hand gestures to ask Johnny why he is hiding. Johnny points towards the problem, so they both go into an empty classroom and hide behind the doors hoping not to be seen.

12 <u>INT. INSIDE A CLASSROOM. ST THOMAS SCHOOL.MUMBAI</u> 12

They both sit down and remain silent for a while and then:

Johnny
My name's Johnny; well, everyone
calls me that. What's yours?

Kid
My name's Raju. Everyone calls
me Rabbit.

Johnny
Rabbit?

Raju
Yeah. Rabbit.

Johnny
Why?

Raju
Cos, I got goofy teeth.

Raju opens his mouth to show Johnny his goofy teeth. The
front teeth are goofy and have a gap between them.

Johnny
Most people call me names too. They call me fatso.
Johnny lifts up his shirt to reveal his oversized belly.

Raju
What's in there?

Johnny

I'm not sure.

Raju pokes Johnny's belly with his finger.

Raju

It's wobbly.

Johnny

Like jelly.

Raju

There's a woman near
my house, who has a
belly like yours. They
say she has a baby inside
her.

Johnny

Do you think I have a
baby inside me?

Raju

I don't know but let me
check.

Raju leans down and listens to Johnny's belly.

Johnny

Can you hear anything?

Raju

There's a grrr grr noise.

Johnny

A grrr grr noise?

Raju

Yes, a grr noise.

Raju pokes Johnny's belly again with his finger and this time, Johnny farts. Both of them start laughing.

Johnny

That's not a grr grrr
noise; that's a boom
noise.

Both of them start laughing and their laughter can be heard outside into the corridor, alerting Big Brother et al to their presence. Shorty and slick burst into the room and drag both Johnny and Raju out into the playground in front of everybody.

13   EXT. SCHOOL PLAYGROUND. ST THOMAS
     SCHOOL.MUMBAI 13

All the school is laughing at them both, and the teachers aren't willing to interfere, fearing that some harm may come to them from the underworld connections these children are linked to.

Big Brother is standing tall, watching over like a predator over its prey.

Shorty (to all)
Looks like a fat boy here
has found himself a
bodyguard.

Slick
A goofy one at that.

Shorty pushes Raju to the ground and grazes; Raju's elbow is beginning to bleed. All the school continues to laugh and shouts: FIGHT, FIGHT, FIGHT, FIGHT!

Johnny walks over and helps Raju up, then stands next to him and looks directly into Big Brother's eyes, which is something you don't do.

This enrages Big Brother.

Big Brother
Right now, we are going to
play a little game.

Big Brother walks over to Raju and asks him to say 'red Lorry; yellow lorry' repeatedly. Raju begins.

Raju
Red lorry; yellow lorry.
Red lorry; yellow lorry.
Red lorry; yellow lolly.

BANG. Big Brother slaps Johnny across the face.

Big Brother

Each time the bodyguard
gets it wrong, the big fat
boss gets it across the face.

Slick to Raju

Carry on, Rabbit, or you'll
have no teeth left.

Raju left with no choice, looks over at Johnny, whose face is still red after the first slap. They both look into each other's eyes with despair realizing there's nothing either of them can do.

Raju

Red lorry; yellow lorry.
Red lorry; yellow lorry.
Red lorry; yellow lorry.
Red lorry; yellow lorry.

Slick to Raju

Faster!

Raju

Red lorry; yellow lorry.
Red lorry; yellow lorry.
Red lolly; yellow lolly.

Everyone laughs as slap after slap hits Johnny across the face. At which point one of the teachers rings the bell for the beginning of the first lesson. Saved by the bell, Johnny and Raju stand in the middle of the yard after being humiliated. Johnny has some blood pouring from his nose as some of the blows were more of a punch than slaps.

Both of them make their way out of school. Raju asks Johnny if he's alright, but Johnny doesn't respond.

Johnny

I'm going home. I'll see
you tomorrow.

Johnny walks down the busy lane as Raju stands there looking at him from a distance. Johnny looks back, and they both acknowledge each other as a tear falls down Johnny's cheek.

14 INT. JOHNNYS SLUM. KAALI BASTI. MUMBAI
14

Johnny walks into his home, and his mum is waiting.

Mum

Hi, Sweety. How is my baby?

Mum kisses Johnny's forehead and doesn't even ask why he has come back home so early or why he has blood over his shirt. Johnny sees that she has been snorting a white powder and still has residues on her nose.

Mum

Baby, do you have any money?

Did you get paid today?

Maa, I was beaten up
at school today?

Mum
Oh no, Baby.

Mum steps out of the house into the alleyway and shouts.

Mum
You bastards! If you
think you can hurt my
Baby, I will fucking kill you!

She then comes back into the house.

Mum
No one's going to hurt
you now, Baby. I've told
'em and scared 'em off.
Now, Baby, I just need
a bit of money as I want
to cook you something nice.

Johnny
I haven't got any.

Mum
What?

51

I haven't got any money.

Mum slaps Johnny and pulls his hair.

Mum
You're useless. I wish
you had never been born.

Somebody then shouts for his mum, and she has to go, so she pushes Johnny out of the way and leaves. Johnny just gets up and sits on his bed whilst crying, looking over at the Muhammad Ali poster on his wall, wishing things would get better for him.

15 EXT. WARRIORS GYM KAALI BASTI.MUMBAI
15

Johnny decides to go to the gym earlier than he normally does as he came back from school early. As he gets there, the gym is locked. So Johnny sits on the steps outside. About an hour later, Mangal arrives with a bag of groceries and newspapers.

Mangal to Johnny
What are you doing here so early?

Johnny doesn't respond as he takes the newspapers from Mangal, allowing him to take the keys out of the pocket to open the gym door.

Mangal asks again as they walk up the stairs.

> Mangal
> How did you get those
> scratches on your nose?

> Johnny
> I was playing football.

> Mangal
> Last time I checked they
> played football with their
> feet and not the nose.

Once in the gym, Mangal switches the lights on and walks to his cabin at the back of the gym.

> Mangal
> No school today?

There is no response from Johnny, who puts the newspapers down.

> Mangal
> Johnny. What's up, son?

> Johnny
> I want to learn how to

box. I want to beat all of
them up.

Johnny is in tears.

Mangal

Who do you want to beat up?

Johnny

They're always making fun
of me and picking on me.

Mangal

Who?

Johnny tells Mangal about the events of the day and how
he is always picked on, and how the teachers don't do
anything because the other kids have fathers and he doesn't.

Mangal

Did you tell your mum?

Johnny

Nods his head to say, "yes."

Mangal

What did she say?

Johnny

She wished I was dead and
hadn't been born.

Johnny tells Mangal about his mother putting white powder up her nose and how she becomes a monster after this. He also tells him how he uses the money he gets from Mangal to survive and fund his mother's drug habit.

Johnny

Teach me how to fight, please?

Mangal

An eye for an eye only ends
up making the whole world
blind. Just forget about it.

Johnny points at the poster of Muhammad Ali.

Johnny

I bet no one messed with him?
As Mangal is about to respond, there's a shout for him.

Mangal

I'm coming.

Mangal to Johnny

I'll be back in two ticks.
Let me go and see what this
guy wants. You wait here.

Johnny walks over to the corner of the cabin, looking at all the boxing memorabilia Mangal has collected over the years. Mangal comes back into the room and sees Johnny looking at his prized possessions.

Mangal walks over to his chair and sits down with his papers and starts to read as Johnny is still looking at the memorabilia. Moments later, Johnny comes and sits next to Mangal on a stool.

Mangal to Johnny
Do you know your mum loves you?

Johnny
She always hits me.

Mangal
That's not her; that's the
Drugs.

Johnny
I don't mean anything to her.
She doesn't care for me. I have no value.

Mangal
You know something. There was
Once this well-known speaker
who started his class
by holding up a five
hundred-rupee bill.
In the room of 200, he asked, "Who would like this 500
rupee bill?"
What do you think happened?
Johnny shrugs his shoulders to say, "I don't know."

Mangal

Hands started going up.
He said, "I am going to give
this 500 rupee to one of you.
But first, let me do this."
He crumpled the 500 rupee bill.
He then asked, "Who still
wants it?"
Still, the hands were up in
the air.
"Well," he replied, "What if
I do this?" and he dropped it
on the ground and started to
grind it in the floor with his
shoe.
He picked it up, now all
crumpled and dirty. "Now who
still wants it." Still the
hands went up in the air.
No matter what he did to
the money, the people still
wanted it because it did
not decrease in value. It
was still worth 500 rupees.
Many times in our lives, we
are dropped, crumpled and
grounded into the dirt by the
circumstances, and we feel as
though we are worthless. But
no matter what has happened
or what will happen, you will

never lose your value.
People who do drugs,
like your mother, don't realize
the effects of what they're
doing has on themselves and
those closest to them. Sometimes,
we have problems, and we all find
it difficult to cope. So we
turn to other things. For some
it's alcohol, and for others, it's
drugs. She's probably going
through a difficult time and
needs help.

<u>Johnny</u>
Can you help her?

<u>Mangal</u>
What makes you think I can
help her?

<u>Johnny</u>
Cos you help everyone and
you're the closest thing to
a dad for me.

There's a long silence. Mangal isn't one known for getting emotional, but those words make him moist-eyed. They both sit there in silence, and then Johnny says:

Johnny

Do you think I have a boy
or a girl?

Mangal

What?

Johnny

In my stomach. Do you think I have a boy or a girl?

Mangal looks confused.

Johnny

My friend Raju said that
if you have a big wobbly
belly like mine, it must
mean I have a baby inside.

Mangal is hysterical and can't contain his laughter. He gets up and hobbles towards Johnny as he rubs his head.

Mangal

Let's go downstairs and I'll
teach you a thing or two.

They both go downstairs and go to the punch-bag. Mangal tells Johnny to punch the bag, which he does. Mangal is disappointed as he can see Johnny is not going to be the next boxing champion, and teaching him to punch properly, let alone box, is going to be a difficult task. As they continue, one of the villagers rushes into the gym.

Villager
(whilst catching his breath)
Chacha, chacha.
(English translation: uncle Uncle)
We need you. Hurry!

Mangal
What is it?

Villager
That drunkard Hari is beating
his wife again.

Mangal
Not again.

Mangal to Johnny
You stay here and don't go
outside.

Johnny nods his head in agreement with Mangal.

Mangal to Villager
Let's go.

Villager
Hurry, hurry!

Mangal
OK, OK, I've only got two legs.

Both of them head out as Mangal asks the villager to close the door behind him. Johnny goes back to the punch-bag and begins to hit it. Whilst muttering, "I'm the champ, I'm the greatest, I'm the greatest," and then tries to do the Ali shuffle and falls over. He picks himself up and heads to the speedball in the corner of the gym; he punches it once but cannot continue the quick succession of punches to keep the momentum going. As he is punching, all of a sudden, a severe thunderstorm—with much hail, rain and thunder—descends upon Kaali Basti. Hail as big as golf balls starts hitting the tin roof of the gym as the water falling on the roof begins to overflow the roof gutters. The sky gets darker and darker. At noon, it's almost as dark as night outside, sometimes split by bright bolts of lightning. Wham! The sky ignites like a flashbulb and simultaneous thunder hits the gym as a gust of wind bangs the gym door open with the rain pouring inside and blowing some of the posters off the wall. Johnny takes off his gloves, runs towards the door and uses all his strength to close the door against the strong gust of wind. Then puts the locks on to ensure it stays closed. He wipes the rain from his face and looks over into the hallway realizing the poster of Muhammad Ali has been blown off the wall. He runs over to pick it up and blows the dust off the poster. Johnny turns back and tries to stick it back on the wall, but he isn't tall enough, so he walks to the other side of the gym to get a chair. He picks up the chair, brings it near to the wall and stands on it to stick the poster back in its original place on the wall. He steps down from the chair and does the Ali shuffle. As Johnny makes his way to the changing rooms, he feels a breeze, but as he turns around, there's nothing there and all the windows and doors are closed. He takes the mop from the changing room and clears the wet floor near the entrance. He takes the mop and puts it back in the changing room. He makes his way back to the punch-bag, puts his gloves back on and starts to punch the bag.

He again feels a breeze, but as he turns around, there's nothing there, and all the windows and doors are closed. As he is punching the bag, a voice from behind says, "Step into it!"

Johnny looks around and to his amazement, sitting on the apron of the ring is none other than Muhammad Ali.

Ali

Well, are you going to punch, kiddo, or just stare?

Johnny just continues to stare.

Ali

Let me show you.

Ali gets off the ring apron and walks towards the punch bag and demonstrates to Johnny how to throw the punch.

Ali

Hold your hand up high
with your elbow in close
to your body. Push off your
back foot. Step forward and
extend your arm straight out
at your target. Rotate your
fist over (thumb inwards) as
you reach full extension.

Drop your chin to your shoulder
to protect your head. Connect
with your hand at the same
time, the toe of your front
foot touches the ground.
Like this.

Ali does a quick succession of punches.

Ali
Let me show you.

Ali holds Johnny and coaches him through the punch and
changes his stance as Johnny punches the bag.

Ali
That's it, Kiddo.

Johnny continues to punch.

Ali
That's it. Let's hear that bag
crying in pain. Bang, Bang!

Johnny continues to punch.

Ali
And again, kiddo.

Johnny continues to punch.

Ali

You're getting good at this.

Johnny

I can punch, Muhammad, I can
punch!

Johnny continues to punch even though he is tired, then
all of a sudden, there's a knock at the gym door. Johnny looks
around, but there's no sign of Ali.

Johnny

Muhammad, Muhammad. Where
are you?

But there's no sign of him.

Mangal

(at the door)
Are you alright in there?

Johnny walks over to open the gym door.

Mangal

What took you so long?

Mangal makes his way in.

Mangal

Why did you lock the door
anyway, son?

Johnny

To keep out the rain.

Mangal

The rain?

Mangal looks at Johnny, not believing him.

Johnny

Yes, the rain. As soon
as you went, it started raining
very bad.

Mangal

Really?

Johnny nods his head to say, "yes."

Mangal

(whilst smiling)
I guess I must be getting
old to have missed that.

Mangal hobbles over towards the stairs.

Mangal to Johnny

Has the?

Then at the door, the milkman arrives.

Mangal to Milkman

Ah, you have a long life.

I was just about to ask of you.

Milkman

Ask about me or curse me?

Mangal

It's the same thing.

As they both laugh. Mangal asks Johnny to take the milk upstairs.

Milkman

I heard Hari came home

drunk again.

Mangal

Yes, he did.

Milkman

He's a drunkard. Did he

beat his wife up?

Mangal

No, the poor soul beat him

up with a bamboo stick. He

was still trying to pull it

out of his behind when I left.

Both of them laugh again.

Mangal

Hey, listen, did it rain earlier?

Milkman

Rain? *Chacha* (uncle) it's not
rained for months.

Mangal

I know, I know. I got up a
little late today and it was
cold in the morning so thought
it may have rained.

Milkman

Not today, *chacha*. I'm off now.

Mangal

Don't forget to pass my regards
to your father. And don't forget
to dilute the milk with more
water.

Milkman

You're always pulling my leg.

Mangal closes the door and goes into the changing room
to wash his face. As he is doing so, he notices the mop by the
sink is wet, but there's no water in the bucket. He follows the
trail of the wet floor back to the gym door, which indicates
there had been a downpour earlier, which both he and the

milkman were oblivious to even though they had been outdoors for most parts of the morning.

Mangal makes his way upstairs, where Johnny, as always, is looking at the tonnes of memorabilia Mangal has collected over the years

Mangal

Are you not going home?

Johnny

Can I stay here a bit longer?

Mangal

How are things at home?

Johnny doesn't say anything but Mangal understands full well how things are at home. Mangal comes and sits on his rocking chair in front of the television as Johnny sits next to him on the floor.

Mangal

Who were you talking to
earlier?

Johnny

When?

Mangal

When I came back from
Hari's?

Johnny

To myself.

Mangal

To yourself?

Johnny changes the topic of conversation quickly.

Johnny

Its Friday tomorrow.

Mangal

It's always Friday after
Thursday.

Johnny

Which fight video are you
going to show me tomorrow?

Mangal

You'll have to wait and
see.

Johnny

Can I come early again
tomorrow?

Mangal

What about school?

Johnny doesn't say anything and shrugs his shoulders.

Mangal

Why do you want to
come early anyway?

Johnny

I want to practice my
Punching.

Mangal

OK. We'll work on your
punching.

Johnny

I can practice on my own.

Mangal

On your own?

Johnny nods his head.

Mangal

OK, kiddo, you can practice
on your own.

17 INT. JOHNNYS SLUM, KAALI BASTI.MUMBAI
17

Johnny rushes home so he can speak to his mum. Upon
arriving there, he finds his mum there with two female friends
of hers, Rani and Sheila.

Rani
(to Mum)
How do you afford to feed him?
Your son must be the fattest
boy in this neighbourhood?

Sheila
(to Rani)
Shut up. You're always having a
go at him. He's just a kid.

Mum
No, she's right. If he controlled
his eating, there probably wouldn't
be any poverty in India.

Rani and Mum laugh.

Sheila
(to Mum)
Stop it. That's your son.

Mum
If you like him so much why
don't you take him home?

Rani and Mum laugh again.

Johnny goes to put his bag down and looks at the poster
of Muhammad Ali. He then stands next to his mum, who is
talking to her friends.

                    Mum
                 What now?

                   Johnny
          I met Muhammad Ali today.

                    Mum
                   Who?

                   Sheila
                 (to Mum)
       Ali is that pimp from downtown.
         Your son is a dark horse.

Rani and Mum laugh again.

                   Johnny
           No, I met Muhammad Ali.
                  today.

Johnny goes and gets the poster of Muhammad Ali off his
wall and shows it to everyone.

                   Johnny
             I met him today.

                    Mum
               You met him?

                   Johnny
                   Yes.

                     72

Both Mum and Rani start laughing hysterically.

Rani

(to Mum)

Your son has gone loopy.

Mum

(whilst pointing to Johnny's head)

He never had anything

in there in the first place.

Both Mum and Rani continue laughing hysterically.

Sheila

(to Mum)

Stop it now.

Johnny walks away with his poster as they continue to laugh and taunt him. Moments later, Johnny comes back.

Mum

What now?

Rani

(to Mum)

He must have met Amitabh Bachan

now (a famous Bollywood actor).

Both Mum and Rani laugh hysterically once again.

Johnny
(to Mum)
Can I have some food?
Please?

Mum
(to friends)
Food, food and food that's all
he ever thinks about. No wonder
he's so fat. Go away!

Johnny
At least give me something. I've
not eaten all day.

Mum
I said, "Go away."

Johnny
Please!

Mum
(slaps Johnny)
I said, "Go away."

Rani laughs as Sheila gets up.

Sheila
(to Johnny)
You come with me.

Rani

(to Mum)

Look at Mother Theresa.

Both Rani and Mum laugh as Sheila walks out with Johnny.

18 INT. SHEILAS HUT, KAALI BASTI.MUMBAI 18
    18

Sheila brings Johnny to her little hut, which she shares with her husband Hari (drunkard) and six-year-old daughter Muskaan (happiness). Johnny treats Muskaan like his younger sister.

Sheila

(to Johnny)

You sit here.

Johnny begins to play with Muskaan whilst Sheila gets a pan and empties out the boiled rice onto a plate. There is only enough rice to fill one person. However, Sheila comes and puts the plate in front of Johnny.

Johnny

(to Sheila)

Is there enough for you
and Muskaan?

Sheila lies to him and says yes. Johnny realises she isn't telling the truth and asks Sheila to come and sit down with him.

Johnny takes some rice and puts it into Sheila's mouth and then feeds Muskaan, making Sheila cry. Then Sheila takes a pinch of rice with her fingers and feeds him. This is the love Johnny yearns for but is unable to get from his own mother.

Johnny

(to Sheila)

I did see Muhammad Ali, you know?

Sheila

(to Johnny)

I believe you.

Johnny

No one else does.

Sheila

Sometimes God sends someone

to watch over you.

Johnny

Like a ghost?

Sheila

Or like an angel.

They both smile as Johnny hugs Sheila, and then all of a sudden, Johnny has a brainwave. He feels the need to tell

Mangal about this as other than Sheila; he's the one who would believe him.

Johnny

(to Sheila)

I've got to go.

Sheila

(to Johnny)

Where? It's raining.

But Johnny runs as fast as he can.

19   EXT. THE STREET. KAALI BASTI.MUMBAI 19

Johnny runs through the water-logged streets in the pouring rain as fast as his overweight body can carry him. Across the potholes, the size of craters and traffic seems to have ballooned severely. As he almost approaches the gym, he is stopped in his tracks by Shorty, Slick and Big Brother.

Big Brother

(to Shorty & Slick)

Now, what do we have here?

Johnny is so out of breath from all the running he is unable to breathe.

Shorty

(to Big Brother)

Looks like the fat boy is tired.

Slick

(to Shorty)

Let's get him a drink of water.

Slick pushes Johnny as he falls into a puddle face first in the pouring rain. Shorty and Slick drag him through the water as Big Brother watches on. After being beaten and humiliated, Big Brother tells Slick and Shorty to stop. Big Brother walks up to Johnny and tells Slick to search his pockets for any money. Slick finds a few coins, which makes them all laugh at Johnny, calling him a beggar.

Slick

(to Big Brother)

What's this?

As he pulls out a folded piece of paper from his shirt pocket. Slick hands the folded paper to Big Brother, who then opens it up to find a picture of Muhammad Ali.

Shorty

Fatso is carrying a picture
of a man. He must be gay.

They laugh at Johnny once again. Big Brother holds the picture up in front of Johnny's face and tears it in half.

Big Brother

(to Johnny)

Even he can't help a loser
like you.

Johnny gets back to his feet as the villagers look on without coming forward to help him in fear of reprisals from the neighbourhood thugs. He looks for the torn picture of Muhammad Ali whilst wiping the tears from his eyes. He finds the torn pieces and makes his way to the gym in the pouring rain.

20   INT. THE WARRIORS GYM. KAALI BASTI.MUMBAI 20

Johnny walks into the gym and there's no sign of Mangal. He calls out for him, but there's no response. He walks over to the poster of Ali and sits on the floor beneath it. He takes out the torn photo and places both pieces on the floor, trying to fit them together like jigsaw pieces. He looks over at the poster.

Johnny
(to Ali's poster)
I wish I was more like you
Mohammad. If I was like you,
I would beat them all up.
No one would mess with me.
Then all of a sudden, a voice from behind says,
"Ain't that a pretty poster?"

Johnny looks round and sees Ali.

Ali
(about his poster)
That was me just before

the second Liston fight.

I was in my prime.

Ali walks over and sees his torn picture on the floor. He picks up the torn photograph and puts the torn pieces into his fist. He rubs the other hand over the fist and then opens up his fist to reveal the complete picture to the amazement of Johnny. Ali gives the photo to Johnny.

Ali

The first time I saw
Corky Baker, he was
holding one of the
football players from
my school's team upside
down, shaking all the
money out of his pockets.
Corky was short, stocky,
had big muscles, a mean
stare and was older than
me. Corky beat up everybody
and terrorised the whole
neighbourhood, including
me. He was mean as he
was strong and had a
reputation for knocking
out grown men. Corky
made money betting on
how high he could lift
the ends of automobiles.
I always walked around

the gym and school
confident and proud,
except when I heard
Corky was on the
streets. Like everybody
else, I had to find
another way around
Corky's block, unless
I wanted to pay the
toll he charged for
the privilege of walking
past him. Corky was
undisputed "King of the
Streets." In almost
every run-in I had
with him, I lost. It
was really staring
to shake me up. Even
with all my training
and boxing skills,
I knew I would never
go far in boxing unless
I stopped Corky Baker.
I thought that if I
could beat Corky, I
could beat the whole
world. I started talking
about how I would whup
Corky if I got him in
the ring. When Corky
found out that I was

going around saying,
he came looking for me.
He said that when he
got his hands on me,
he was going to tear
me apart.
When I confronted him,
Corky wanted to fight me
right then and there,
but I knew it would be
suicide to fight him
in the streets without
any rules or regulations
and no referee. So I
challenged Corky to
a boxing match at
they gym. Corky laughed
and said boxing was for
sissies that it wasn't
real fighting. But when
everybody started
laughing at him and
calling him a coward,
Corky quickly changed
his mind and accepted.
When the day of the
fight arrived I was
scared to death, but I
had my father and my
brother with me. All my
friends from the

neighbourhood and classmates were there. It was time for the showdown. Corky and I were about to fight three rounds for the title that would mean the most to me. Whoever won this fight would be the "King of the Street." I couldn't see myself as a real champion until I stood up to Corky. As I stood in my corner of the ring. I hoped that Corky wouldn't notice my knees were shaking. When the bell rang for the first round, I came out moving, throwing jabs then tried to stay out of his reach. Corky came out swinging. He was throwing big hard punches that weren't landing. I kept moving because if Corky hit me, he would have knocked me out. But Corky was quickly becoming tired.

When the bell rang for
the second round, Corky
came out chasing me but
he couldn't catch me. I
was ducking his punches,
and I was faster and
smarter than he was.
Before the second round
was over, he said, "This
isn't fair," and ran out
of the ring and left
the gym. I had won the
respect and the title.
I had blackened his eye
and bloodied his nose.
More importantly, I had
faced my fear and gained
the self-respect and self-
confidence I needed
to continue my boxing
career. For a while, I
walked around the
neighbourhood, looking
over my shoulder. I thought
Corky might come after me.
But he didn't and I was
surprised by what he said
to me when I did see him
again. He told me that I
was a good fighter and that
I was going to go a long way.

He shook my hand and walked
off.

<u>Johnny</u>
What happened to Corky?

<u>Ali</u>
Over the years, Corky
and I kind of became friends
and he kept up with all my
fights. After Ken Norton broke
my jaw, I thought about Corky.
I called up an old friend
who had grown up next door
to me back in Louisville.
I asked him where Corky was
now; I wanted to hear what
he thought of my fight with
Norton. But I didn't get a
chance to talk to Corky.
My friend told me that Corky
was dead. Just a few weeks
before I called, Corky was in
a shootout with police at a
bar in Louisville. I still
think of Corky. He reminds me
of what can be accomplished if
we face our fears.
You need to stand up to
those guys that did all
this to you.

Then Mangal arrives.

> Mangal
> Hey, kiddo, why are you
> sitting on the floor?

Johnny looks back at him and then points towards Ali, but he seems to have disappeared.

> Mangal
> Are you OK? I heard
> what happened.

> Johnny
> I just wanted to come
> and tell you about Muhammad
> because I know you
> would believe me.

> Mangal
> Muhammad?

> Johnny
> Yes, Muhammad.

Mangal isn't sure which Muhammad Johnny is talking about. Johnny then points to the poster of Ali.

> Mangal
> Ah, OK? What about him?

Johnny
He was here.

Mangal
Here?

Johnny
Yes.

Mangal
He was here?

Johnny
Yes.

Mangal
In my gym?

Johnny
Yes.

Mangal
Now let me get this
straight. Muhammad
Ali previously known
As Cassius Clay. Three
times World Heavyweight
Champion
Was here in this gym?

Johnny
Yes.

Mangal
Out of all the places
he could go to, he came
to this gym in Mumbai.

Johnny
Well, yeah.

Mangal
Why?

Johnny
I don't know.

Mangal
Come here.

Mangal feels Johnny's forehead.

Mangal
You haven't got a
Temperature, have you?
As I think you are
seeing things.

Johnny
I'm not. He was here.

Mangal

So, where is he now?

Johnny

He disappeared.

Mangal

I think it's time for
you to disappear as
well because it's getting
late.

Johnny

Honestly, I'm telling
the truth.

Mangal

OK, so what did he say?

Johnny

He told me that I
should face my fears.

Mangal

Face your fears?

Johnny

Yes.

Mangal

OK, son. I think you

should go home and
get some rest as I
think those guys have
given you brain damage.

Johnny
I'm telling the truth.
Honestly.

Mangal
Yeah, yeah.

Mangal hands Johnny an umbrella and tells him to go straight home.

Johnny
Wait a minute. He told
me about how he was
bullied by Candy Baker
and how he stood up to him.
How would I know that?

Mangal doesn't respond.

Johnny
I always thought if
nobody else believes
me, you would.

Johnny leaves the gym disappointed.

Johnny makes his way home in the pouring rain and is confronted by Big Brother and some of his adult thugs.

<u>Big Brother</u>
So let's see some of
your boxing moves.

Johnny is surrounded by the gang, who once again assault him and push him to the ground. They take his umbrella and throw it in the air, which is caught by Mangal.
Mangal walks up to the thugs.

<u>Mangal</u>
How about you pick on
somebody your own size?

Mangal then uses the umbrella to beat up the adult thugs and then turns to Big Brother.

<u>Mangal</u>
How do you like the
boxing moves?

Mangal straightens the collar of Big Brother, who looks worried.

<u>Mangal</u>
Now run along and go to
your daddy. Have a nice
evening, son.

Mangal walks over to Johnny and opens the umbrella.

Mangal

Come on, kiddo. Let me
walk you home.

Mangal stands singing the lyrics to the song, 'I'm singing in the rain' by Gene Kelly.

Mangal

I'm singing in the rain
Just singing in the rain
What a glorious feelin'
I'm happy again.
I'm laughing at clouds.
So dark up above
The sun's in my heart
And I'm ready for love
Let the stormy clouds
Chase
Everyone from the place
Come on with the rain
I've a smile on my face
I walk down the lane
With a happy refrain
Just singin'
Singin in the rain

22   INT. JOHNNYS HUT. KAALI BASTI.MUMBAI 22

Both Mangal and Johnny arrive at Johnny's hut.

Mum

(to Johnny)

Where the hell have you
been? And whose this
old man with you?

She walks back into the house, lights a cigarette and starts
smoking.

Mangal

(to Johnny)

Aren't you going to
ask your son how he is
or why he is covered
in mud? Aren't you
going to ask him why
he's late or why he's
bleeding?

Mum

(to Mangal)

Who are you and what are you doing here?

Johnny

(to Mum)

This is Mangal.

Mum

(to Mangal)

Well, you can go now.

Mangal begins to walk towards the door and then turns back.

Mangal

(to Mum)

I wanted to see for

Myself.

Mum

(to Mangal)

What?

Mangal

(to Mum)

Do you know what a

mother is?

Mum

(to Mangal)

What?

Mangal

(to Mum)

A mother is someone to

shelter and guide us,

who love us, whatever we

do with a warm

understanding and

infinite patience

and wonderful

gentleness, too.

How often a mother

means swift reassurance
in soothing our small,
childish fears.
How tenderly mothers
watch over their
children and treasure
them all through the
years. The heart of a
mother is full of
forgiveness. For any
mistake, big or small,
and generous always
in helping her family,
whose needs she has
placed above all.
A mother can utter a
word of compassion
and make all our
cares fall away.
She can brighten a
home with the sound
of her laughter
and make life delightful.
A mother possesses
incredible wisdom
and wonderful insight
and skill. In each
human heart is that
one special corner
which only a mother
can fill.

That's what a mother is.

Mum
(to Mangal)
How many mums have a
son like that?

Mangal
He's got a junkie for
a mother. How many sons
have a mum like that?
If you walked by a
street and you saw a
rose growing from
concrete or mud, even
if it had messed up
petals, and it was
a little to the side,
you would marvel at
just seeing a rose
grow through concrete.
So why is it that
when you see some
slum kid grow
out of the dirtiest
circumstance and he
can talk, he can
sit across the room, make you cry,
make you laugh and all
you can talk about
is his dirty stems and

how he's leaning
crooked to the side.
You can't even see
that he's come up
from out of all this.
He is what you made him.
I don't know what you
have been through but
it's time to sort
yourself out and be a
mother. No matter how
grown-up you think
he is, we all need
our mothers because
one good mother
is worth a hundred
schoolmasters.

Mangal makes his way out of the house as Johnny is being hugged by his mother. He turns back to Johnny.

Mangal
His name was Corey Baker.

Johnny
Whose?

Mangal
That bully Mohammad fought
was called Corey, not Candy.

Mangal winks at Johnny, who is happy knowing that Mangal believes him.

23   INT. WARRIOR'S GYM. KAALI BASTI.MUMBAI 23

It's a sunny day without a single cloud in the sky. It's a rare beautiful thing without a breeze. Mangal is in the gym watching his regulars working out. He is watching two guys sparring in the ring as he watches on from the ropes.

Mangal

Stop, stop, come here.

Both guys walk over to the ropes where Mangal is standing.

Mangal

Are you best friends?

Both nod their heads to say, "no."

Mangal (to the first guy)

Is he your boyfriend?

Guy 1

Hell no!

Mangal (to the second guy)

Is he your lover?

<u>Guy 2</u>
I'm not a homo!

<u>Mangal</u>
So why the hell have you been
hugging each other for the
last three rounds? If you're not
going to hit each other, you may
as well put your tongue down each other's
throats. Now let's see some jabs
and combinations.

Both men go back to their sparring as Mangal continues to watch with an eagle eye. Then all of a sudden, two muscular men, both over six feet tall, burst into the gym and start shouting.

"Right, everyone out. Work-outs
Over!"

Both men start pushing everyone towards the exit whilst pointing and shouting abuse at them and slapping and kicking those who are slow to respond.

Mangal stays standing on the edge of the ring apron as they empty the gym.

Then one of the men picks up a chair, places it in the centre of the ring and stands there staring at Mangal as the other man goes to the door. The man standing in the ring lights a cigarette and starts smoking. He then walks over to Mangal on the ring apron and exhales the smoke in his face whilst smirking. The man at the door then indicates to him that the boss is here

The boss is the *Bhai* (the word linguistically means brother; however, in Mumbai slang, it means underworld gangster)

The man in the ring drops the cigarette whilst putting it out with his foot.

Then in walks the boss, followed by four men, two on each side. The boss is a tallish dark-skinned man with a moustache wearing sunglasses and a scar going down the right-hand side of his face. There is sparkle from the many gold rings he is wearing on both hands and a gold chain around his neck. He walks towards the ring as one of the men lifts the rope for him to get into the ring and he goes and sits on the chair in the middle of the ring.

The boss points at Mangal and laughs.

<u>The Boss</u>
This is him.

The henchmen confirm by saying, "Yes, Boss."

<u>The Boss</u>
Hey, old man. Have mercy
on your old bones. You don't
want to overdo it at your age.

<u>Mangal</u>
A guy at my age has seen
many like you come and go.

The boss stands up and walks up to Mangal, takes off his sunglasses and looks directly into the eyes.

The Boss
Many like me?

Mangal
Do you know what a leech is?

There is a pin-drop silence and a confused look on the face of the boss.

Mangal
It's something that clings on to
others and preys on something
weaker, sucking on its blood.

The Boss
You got a big mouth for an
old man.

Mangal
And a big everything else too?

The boss laughs.

The Boss
The world heavyweight champion
here thinks he has a big set
of balls. It's a shame they
don't work, which is probably

why his wife died as she wasn't
getting no action.

The boss and his men start laughing.

The Boss
So, is that why you're so
frustrated and angry because
you're impotent and you can't
have children.

Mangal
Maybe you should go ask
your mother that as she
wasn't complaining last night.

The boss slaps Mangal across the face and grabs him by
the collar.

The Boss
I'm going to play
on your fears and make you
regret the day you were born. You'll never be the same
again, my friend. It's a
matter of time, you'll never
rest easy again. You'll know it's coming, you won't
know how or when; you'll
have to watch and wait.
You know, it feels
intoxicating to be
intimidating. It's

invigorating to see you
shaking. You know something,
you see it coming and you
know I will stop at nothing.

Mangal
Well, I know you're not stupid
enough to make a scene
with all these people here.
What would that do for your
reputation? A gangster
beating up a 72-year-old man.

The boss lets go of Mangal's collar and straightens them out. He then walks back and sits on the chair in the middle of the ring and continues to smoke.

The Boss
You messed with my kid
last night for some slumdog.
Do you know what can happen
to you or how powerful I am?

Mangal
He is the most powerful who
has power over himself.

The Boss
Power takes a back-step only
in the face of more power, and
when I look at you, I see an

old man whistling in the dark.
Around here, you will do what I
say. Jump when I say jump, take
a shit when I say you take a shit.

Mangal
You say you're powerful. But
being powerful is like being a
lady. If you have to tell
people you are, maybe you aren't.
Maybe you are the whore that
gets banged every night.

The henchmen of the boss try to attack Mangal, but the boss signals them to step down as he gets up from the chair and walks up to Mangal again.

The Boss
You're a hot-headed bastard, aren't you?

The boss continues to smoke, exhaling the smoke on Mangal's face.

The Boss
I don't normally crush ants
until they are ready to bite,
but this one seems to have
a sting in its tail. I'm
going to enjoy crushing you.

The boss climbs out of the ring with his men and makes
way to the exit and Mangal hobbles behind them.

The Boss
Take care old man. Health
can be very fragile at your
age.

The boss straightens Mangal's collar on his shirt.

Mangal
Tell your boys to leave
the kid alone.

Mangal removes the hands of the boss from his shirt.

The Boss
I'm the one that does the
telling. Not him, not him
and not you.

Mangal
Let's settle this once and for all.

The Boss
Ha Ha. I've got to give it to
You, old man. You have got guts.
But like I said, I'm the one
that does the telling around
here.

Mangal

Everyone calls you *Bhai* and
They say you're a man of your
word.

The Boss

Your point is?

Mangal

The kid was outnumbered.
Let's make it fair.

The Boss

How?

Mangal points at the Amateur Boxing Tournament poster on the wall near the exit.

Mangal

Your boy against mine.

The boss starts laughing hysterically, as do his men.

The Boss

As well as being old and
senile you have become a
bit of a comedian in your old
age.

The boss and his men continue to laugh.

Mangal

Are you scared?

There is a pin-drop silence and the boss squares up to Mangal.

The Boss

You or the boy better not
even think about running
away because I have eyes
everywhere.

Mangal

And the boy is left alone
to train?
The boss shouts over to his men.

The Boss

No one touches the old man or the boy.
Then he looks over at Mangal.
You're on.

24 INT. WARRIOR'S GYM. KAALI
BASTI.MUMBAI 24

Hours later, Johnny walks into the gym after school and is very excited. Mangal is reading the newspaper whilst sitting on the edge of the ring apron.

Johnny

So?

Mangal
So what?

Johnny
Its Friday.

Mangal
Well done. Did you figure
that out all by yourself or
did someone help you with
that?

Johnny
So what fight are we
watching today?

Mangal
You mister are watching
no fight.

Johnny
Why?

Mangal
Well, because you haven't
done your homework yet.

Johnny
I have no homework.

Mangal
Really?

Johnny
Honestly.

Mangal
Why not?

Johnny
I'm tired of doing homework.

Mangal
Hard work never killed anyone.

Johnny
I know, but I don't want to
be the first.

Mangal just looks at Johnny, not taking in any of his
excuses.

Johnny
I have so much homework
to finish. The teacher
said she might send someone
to my home.

Mangal
To talk to your mum?

Johnny
No, to help me carry it
to school.

Mangal
No excuse is going to
work, kiddo.

Johnny
It takes me about two hours
each night to do my homework.
Four if my mum helps me.

Mangal
It's a shame you won't do
your homework because I was
going to…

Mangal continues reading his newspaper whilst stopping
in the middle of the sentence.

Johnny
You were going to?

Mangal
Watch this small fight.

Johnny
Which small fight?

Mangal
Rumble in…

Johnny
The jungle.

Mangal nods his head to say, "yes."

Mangal
It's a shame you won't do
your homework otherwise
you could have watched it
with me.

Without saying a word Johnny goes and sits down in the corner with his bag. He takes his books out and begins doing his homework as quickly as possible as he'll do anything to watch Muhammad Ali. About an hour has passed when Johnny walks up to Mangal with his homework book.

Mangal
All done?

Johnny
Yes.

Johnny hands over his book to Mangal to show him the completed homework.

Mangal

OK, let's go.

Johnny runs and locks the doors and turns off the lights downstairs. They both head upstairs. Johnny hears some noises but thinks nothing of them in his excitement.

25 <u>RUMBLE IN THE JUNGLE. INSIDE WARRIORS GYM.</u> 25

Mangal put's the VHS tape into the video recorder and presses the rewind button. As the videotape rewinds, Mangal sets the scene for Johnny by giving him an insight into the fight that was the "Rumble in the Jungle."

Mangal

On the morning of October
30th 1974, Muhammad Ali
was just hours away from
entering the ring to challenge
undisputed heavyweight
Champion George Foreman.
The fight with Foreman
represented more than just
a chance for him to become
the second former heavyweight
champ to regain the title.
A victory over Foreman meant
redemption for Ali.
By October 1974, seven years
had passed since Ali was
stripped off his heavyweight

title for refusing Induction
into the U.S. Army on April
28th 1967. After the then
Cassius Clay defeated Sonny
Liston in February of 1964
to capture the heavyweight
title, he announced that he
was a member of the Nation
of Islam and was adopting
the name Cassius X. Two weeks
later he was given the name
Muhammad Ali by Elijah Muhammad,
the leader of the Nation of
Islam. From that point on,
Ali was a marked man by the
so-called establishment and
viewed as someone dangerous
and capable of sighting
a race war between Whites and
Blacks.
After a 43 month forced exile
from boxing, Ali returned to
the ring. In the four years
in between his comeback fight
with Jerry Quarry in October
1970, up to his title fight
with George Foreman in October
1974, Ali fought for the title
once and went 12–2 in 14 fights.
In his first title shot, he
lost a 15 round unanimous

decision to undefeated Heavyweight Champion Joe Frazier in the biggest and most anticipated fight in boxing history. After losing to Frazier, Ali won ten fights in a row against the top contenders in the heavyweight division. In an effort to force Frazier into fighting him again, he was trying to eliminate all of his future opponents. In his eleventh the fight he was upset by seventh ranked contender Ken Norton. Norton won a split decision over Ali and broke his jaw in the fight. The loss to Norton was the low point of Ali's career. Two months before Ali lost to Norton, George Foreman demolished Joe Frazier in two rounds to become undisputed heavyweight champion. With Foreman's win over Frazier, coupled with Ali's loss to Norton, Ali was perceived as being fourth in the pecking order among the four.

Six months after losing to

Norton, Ali fought him again
and won the rematch by a split
decision to even the score.
Four months later, Ali won
a unanimous decision over
the only other fighter to
defeat him, Joe Frazier,
knotting them at 1–1. Two
months after Ali beat
Frazier, Foreman knocked out
Norton in the second round
to retain the heavyweight title
in Caracas, Venezuela. To
insure Foreman didn't have
the spotlight all to himself,
Ali was ringside for the fight.
Foreman hadn't even had his
arms raised in victory and
Ali was already in the ring
issuing challenges to him.
The drumbeat for Foreman vs Ali
started immediately afterwards.
And it was the antics of Ali
that kept the fight front and
center for the next couple of
months. The only thing missing
was someone to come up with
the money needed to make the
fight.
When a new promoter on the
Scene, named Don King, showed

up with 10 million dollars
for Foreman and Ali to split
(the largest purse in the history
at the time), the fight was made.

Johnny
Is he that man with a funny hairstyle?

Mangal
That's the one. The fight was
set for 1974 in Kinshasa, Zaire.

Johnny
Where's that?

Mangal
It's in Africa somewhere.

Johnny
Is that far?

Mangal
Very.

Johnny
Do you have to get a bus to
get there?

Mangal (whilst laughing)
Yes you have to get many buses.

The videotape has stopped. Mangal asks Johnny to press the play button as he sits on the rocking chair. Johnny presses the button; however, the tape hasn't rewound fully.

Mangal
It's only gone to halfway, kiddo.
You need to press stop and then
rewind, so it goes to the beginning.

As the videotape continues to rewind, Mangal continues painting a picture of the pre-fight hype.

Mangal
For Ali, beating Foreman
would signify his redemption
after having the title
taken away from him for
political reasons seven
years earlier. However,
Foreman was thought to
be so unbeatable and
invincible at the time.
Ali, then 32, wasn't given
much of a chance against
him. But Muhammad Ali was
at his brilliant best when
pushed to the edge of a
cliff. And he realized that
if he could beat Foreman,
his detractors and critics
would have to pay homage

to him and admit he was
an all-time great heavyweight
champion.
The George Foreman of 1974,
who Ali confronted, was
thought to be the single
greatest puncher in heavyweight
history.
His eight fights prior
to fighting Ali ended in the
first or second rounds.
The question wasn't if
Foreman was going to beat
Ali, that was assumed.
It was just how long
would it take and how
much punishment would
Ali absorb in the process?
The most respected fight
observers in the world
couldn't envision any
fighter withstanding
Foreman's fierce assault.
Former heavyweight champions,
Joe Louis and Jack Dempsey,
both said they'd never
seen a fighter who could
hit like Foreman and
gave Ali no chance to
win. And stated that Ali
no longer had the legs

to stay away and box
Foreman. They were both
certain Ali couldn't win
and would be overwhelmed
by the champion's awesome
strength and punching power.
Some felt that maybe the
Ali of the sixties, who
had great legs and the
ability to move laterally,
may have been able to
stay away from Foreman
and outbox him, but not
the Ali of 1974. Since
returning to the ring
against Quarry, Ali's
legs only resembled
their pre-exile form in
his rematch with Ken
Norton and that only
lasted for the first six
rounds in their 12 round
bout. Holding off Foreman
for 15 rounds figured to
be much tougher.
The Ali travelling show
arrived in Zaire shortly
before Foreman did, a month
before the original date
of September 25th. Before
Ali's feet were firmly

planted on the African
soil, he began to win
the crowd over, leading
to the chant 'Ali, *bomaye*'
(Ali, kill him).
A week before the fight
in the last round of his
sparring session, Foreman
was cut over his eye.
The fight had to be pushed
back to October 30th.
The dictator at that
time, Mobutu Sese Seko—
reportedly the seventh
richest man in the world—
ordered both fighters
to remain in the country.
Since it was his government
that put up the ten
million dollars for the
fight, he didn't want to
chance the fighters leaving
and not coming back. It
was well known that
Foreman hated being there
and wanted to leave, and
it came out years later
that Ali wanted to leave
almost as bad.
Finally, after a five-week
postponement, October

30th arrived with the
fight set to start at 4 am.
This early morning start
was so the fight could be
seen on closed-circuit TV
broadcast in the U.S.
Ali, the challenger, came
to the ring first. Foreman
took his time leaving his
dressing room in an attempt
to throw Ali off. And just
as he used the postponement
of the fight to his
advantage, Ali used this
extra time to get the crowd
worked up in showing their
support of him. After keeping
Ali waiting for about eight
minutes, Foreman came storming
out of his dressing room jogging
towards the ring.
At the center ring, they both
attempted to stare the other
down. While Referee Zack
Clayton was giving the
instructions, Ali said to
Foreman, "You've been hearing
about me since you were a
boy in diapers and now you
have to face me; you're
in trouble." Foreman just

glared back at Ali and
both fighters went back
to their corner to wait
for the bell to ring for
round one. Ali constantly
said, leading up to the fight,
that he knew he had to beat
Foreman to prove he is the
greatest. And that if he
lost to Foreman, he lost
his right to ever proclaim
himself the greatest. He
also said he was going to
dance and box Foreman
in the fight.

The tape stops; Johnny runs over and plays the tape as he sites it in front of the small television. The bell rings for round one; Ali flew out of his corner and met Foreman almost in his corner. In the first round, Foreman was on top of Ali and forcing him to fight. The only thing saving Ali was his quicker hands, enabling him to beat Foreman to the punch disrupting his charge briefly and his cast-iron chin when he was caught flush.

From about mid-second round on, Ali became stationary and used the ropes to lean back and catch Foreman's bombs on his arms, shoulders and body. What Ali found out in those early rounds was Foreman cut the ring off better than he thought, but the ring surface was soft and slowed him down. And lastly, after being hit with some of Foreman's bombs, he thought if he could weather Foreman's early assault, the payoff could be an exhausted champion in the later rounds.

From rounds three to seven, Foreman stalked Ali and tried to take his head off with every punch he threw. As Foreman bored in to try and work Ali over, Ali would time him catching him with quick straight lefts and rights, and every once in a while, he'd nail him with right-hand leads. When Foreman had Ali on the ropes, he unloaded on him with every big punch in his arsenal. While Ali was getting hammered, he talked to Foreman, telling him to hit harder and saying things like, "Is that all you got," or "That didn't hurt."

At the end of the seventh round, Foreman was tired. He came out for the eighth round and tried to remain the aggressor and continued taking the fight to Ali. In turn, Ali went to the ropes as he had in the rounds before. At the end of the eighth round, Ali caught an overextended Foreman with a left-right followed by another stinging one-two, the last punch a straight right to Foreman's jaw sent him to the canvas. Foreman just missed beating the count of ten, not that it would've made a difference since he had nothing left and was ruled out by Referee Zack Clayton waving his hands signalling the end of the fight. The waving of Clayton's hands marked the end of Foreman's title tenure and began Ali's second. Ten years after beating Sonny Liston, Ali was heavyweight champion of the world again. Ali's knockout of Foreman did much more than just get back the title he was stripped of seven years earlier. What it did was validate him as a great fighter, something he'd been saying since the early sixties. Against Foreman, Ali did what was deemed impossible by every respected boxing expert/observer alive, win.

Johnny is sitting there in amazement and mesmerised by what he just witnessed.

Mangal

That was it, kiddo. The Rumble
in the Jungle.
On October 30th, 1974, Muhammad
Ali defeated George Foreman
because he was as tough or
tougher than any fighter who
has yet lived. And that is
also why he beat Joe Frazier.
To say it was Ali's skill as
a boxer that carried him to
victory is a complete myth.
Against Foreman and Frazier,
Ali wasn't able to slide and
glide to stay out of harms way.
He fought flatfooted against
them because he no longer had
the legs that he used to move
like he did against Sonny Liston.
That's how you know it was
Ali's toughness and durability
that enabled him to defeat
Frazier and Foreman, more
than his skill as a boxer.
Had Ali not been so tough
and blessed with a steel
chin, he would've been
stopped by both. Ali out

boxed Sonny Liston, he out
fought Joe Frazier and
George Foreman.
Ali had told his trainer,
Angelo Dundee, and his
fans that he had a secret plan
for Foreman. As the second
round commenced, Ali
frequently began to lean
on the ropes and cover-up,
letting Foreman punch him
on the arms and body
(a strategy Ali later
dubbed the rope-a-dope).
As a result, Foreman spent
his energy throwing punches
that either did not hit Ali
or were deflected in a way
that made it difficult for
Foreman to hit Ali's head,
while sapping Foreman's
strength due to the large
number of punches thrown
by the champion. This loss
of energy was the key to
Ali's 'rope-a-dope' tactic.

Johnny
I wish I was like him.

Mangal

Like who?

Johnny

Muhammad Ali.

Mangal

What would you do if you
ever had to box?

Johnny

I don't know how to.

Mangal

You could learn.

Johnny

I'm too fat.

Mangal

You could still learn.

Johnny

I prefer eating.

Mangal

Anyways, kiddo, you better
go home. It's getting late.

Johnny grabs his bag and makes his way out.

                    Mangal
                    Hey, kiddo.

                    Johnny
                    Yeah?

                    Mangal
            It's OK. Nothing. I'll tell
                 you tomorrow.

                    Johnny
                OK, see you.

Johnny makes his way home whilst chanting Ali's motto:
"Float like a butterfly, sting like a bee, his hands can't hit what
his eyes can't see. Float like a butterfly, sting like a bee."

26 INSIDE WARRIORS GYM. 26

Johnny makes his way into the gym and starts sweeping
the floor as Mangal is training the boxers. Once he is finished,
he comes and watches Mangal training the other boxers.

                    Johnny
           Something unusual happened
                    today.

                    Mangal
                  Oh, yeah?

Johnny
Yeah.

Mangal
Well…

Johnny
Well, what?

Mangal
What's this unusual thing
that happened to you?

Johnny
I wasn't bullied today.
They said something about
me only having a few weeks
before they got their hands
on me.

Mangal
Oh, yeah. I was going to tell
you yesterday.

Johnny
Tell me what?

Mangal
There's a boxing tournament
next month.

Johnny
Ah, OK.

Mangal
The one that happens every year.

Johnny
Ah, OK.

Mangal
The one that kid always wins
who bullies you.

Johnny
Ah, OK.

Mangal
I signed you up for the
Tournament.

Johnny
Ah, OK.

Then all of a sudden Johnny just realises what Mangal just said.

Johnny
You did what?

Mangal
I signed you up for that
tournament next month.

Johnny
Why?

Mangal
It will stop you from getting
a beating for a while.

Johnny
But I'm going to get beaten
up badly at the tournament.

Mangal
Well, at least, you will get
away with it this month.

Johnny
I'm dead. Why did you
sign me up for this?

Mangal
I was trying to help.

Johnny
Help?

Mangal
Yes, help.

Johnny
How is this going to help?
I'm so dead.

<u>Mangal</u>
You can train.

<u>Johnny</u>
How?

<u>Mangal</u>
I will help you.

<u>Johnny</u>
But how are you going to
stop him from beating me.

<u>Mangal</u>
You won't get beaten up.

<u>Johnny</u>
How is that so?

<u>Mangal</u>
Simple. You beat him up
first.

<u>Johnny</u>
Oh, great. I'm so dead.
He's going to kill me.
He's going to hurt me this
Time.

Johnny is so hysterical and can't believe what Mangal has got him into.

Mangal
Hey, listen.

Johnny
I'm so dead.

Mangal
Hey, listen, kiddo.

Mangal grabs Johnny by the shoulders and shakes him whilst Johnny is almost in tears.

Mangal
Listen. It's time to face
your fears.

Johnny
But he's going to kill me.

Mangal
Not if you stand up to him.

Johnny
How?

Mangal
Float like a butterfly.
Sting like a bee.

Johnny
I'm scared.

<u>Mangal</u>
Don't you think Ali was
scared when he fought Foreman?

<u>Johnny</u>
Maybe.

<u>Mangal</u>
Don't you think Ali was
scared when he fought Liston?

<u>Johnny</u>
Maybe.

<u>Mangal</u>
He was. It's natural to be
scared.

<u>Johnny</u>
I can't fight, though.

<u>Mangal</u>
I will train you.

<u>Johnny</u>
He's too strong.

<u>Mangal</u>
So?

<u>Johnny</u>
I can't beat him.

<u>Mangal</u>
You don't know that.
You may never know what
Results may come of your
action, but if you do
nothing, there will be no
result.

<u>Johnny</u>
I can't fight, though.

<u>Mangal</u>
I will train you.

<u>Johnny</u>
He's too strong.

<u>Mangal</u>
Remember a few days ago,
you said you saw Ali, right?
Here and he told you to
face your fears.

<u>Johnny</u>
Yes.

<u>Mangal</u>
Well, now's the time to

134

stand up. This guy is
your Corey Baker and you
need to whup his ass like
Ali did.

Johnny (reluctantly)
OK.

Mangal
Now go home and get some
rest and be here after school
tomorrow and we will start
training.

On his way home, Johnny passes by his friend's (Raju's) house. He walks up to the window and starts making animal noises. This is the signal for Raju to come out. A few minutes later, Raju appears with some bruises on his face.

Johnny
What happened?

Raju
I fell.

Johnny
From where?

Raju
The moon.

Johnny
The moon?

Raju (laughs)
Not really.

Both of them walk to a spot where they normally sit. From here, they can see the whole city in the distance. Raju is struggling to sit still with the pain.

Johnny
Are you OK?
Raju says yes with his mouth whilst nodding his head to say, "no," and they both laugh.

Johnny
I'm fighting in the tournament.

Raju
Which tournament?

Johnny
The boxing tournament.

Raju
Are you scared?

Johnny
Very.

Raju

If anyone can win, you

can.

Johnny

Do you think so?

Raju

I know so.

Johnny smiles as he put his hands around Raju, and they look down onto the city.

27 INSIDE WARRIORS GYM. TRAINING (Week 1)

27

Johnny walks into the gym, and soon as he put his bag down, Mangal takes him by the hand and walks him over to the corner of the gym, where there is a skipping rope.

Mangal

Well, there you go. I want

you to start skipping. Any

questions?

Before Johnny can respond.

Mangal

Right. Let the training

begin!

Mangal goes onto keeping an eye on everything around the gym as Johnny struggles to do the skipping. Every few minutes, Mangal comes over and shows Johnny how he should be doing the skipping whilst passing on words of encouragement, but he knows this is an impossible task ahead. Hours have passed, and now Johnny is with Mangal doing sit-ups.

<u>Mangal</u>
Come on, Johnny boy, two.
One and a quarter, one and
A half, one and three quarters.
And two. Two, Johnny boy, two.

Johnny struggles to complete two sit-ups, and the look of disappointment can be seen on his face, whilst other people in the gym can be seen jeering and smirking.

<u>Mangal</u>
Don't worry, kiddo. It's only
the first day. You will get
better. I want you to start
training in the evening when
there is nobody here so you
can focus and not feel
embarrassed.
I think that's enough for
Your first day. How are you
feeling?

Johnny

All my body is hurting.

Mangal (laughs)

This is only the beginning, kiddo.
So get used to that feeling.
I'm off. Do you want me to
walk you home?

Johnny

I'll be OK.

Mangal

In that case, just put all the
ropes in the basket and turn
the lights off once you're done.
I'll see you tomorrow after school.

Mangal makes his way out of the gym whilst Johnny starts to tidy the place. Whilst doing this, there is a power cut with only the light shining in from the huge windows from the street lights outside. Johnny continues to tidy up the gym. He sees that the skipping rope he was using is still on the floor. He walks over to the rope, and there's a noise.

Johnny

Who is it?

There is no response, and Johnny is frightened. Johnny walks over to where the noise came from and arms himself with a folded newspaper on the way.

Johnny
Who is it?

A cat jumps out of nowhere, making Johnny scream, but when he realises it's a cat, he begins to laugh. Johnny takes the cat and pushes it out through the door. He then makes his way back to put the skipping rope away. When Johnny goes back, he finds that the skipping rope is missing. He had only left it on the floor moments ago, but it's not there now. Johnny begins to look for the rope in the dark and gets down on his hands and knees. He moves his hands around whilst on his knees, trying to find the skipping rope. As he is doing so, he looks up, staring through the huge windows into the streetlights, and he sees a shadow of a man hopping up and down.

Man
I love skipping. Keeps
me fit and keeps me light
on my toes.

As the streetlights shine on the shadow, Johnny realises it is Muhammad Ali. Johnny watches him as he skips like no one else Johnny has seen skipping before.

Ali
That was good.

Ali takes the skipping rope, brings it over to Johnny and shows him how to skip. Johnny, knowing he can't skip, is reluctant, so Ali asks him to close his eyes. Upon doing so,

Ali passes through Johnny, and as Johnny opens his eyes, he begins to skip.

Johnny (hysterically)
Moham. Look, I can skip; I can skip.

Ali
You're almost as good as me.

Then all of a sudden, the electricity comes back, and Mangal is back. Johnny runs over to Mangal and cannot get his words out.

Mangal
You still here?

Johnny looks back to see Ali dancing in the ring and tries to get Mangal's attention. But Mangal is busy looking at his newspaper.

Johnny
I want to show you something.

Mangal
What is it?

Johnny
Hurry up. Look, look!

As Johnny points over to the ring, it is empty and there is nothing there.

Mangal

What am I supposed to be
looking at?

Johnny is lost for words and doesn't know how to explain
what he saw earlier.

Mangal

What is it, kiddo?

Johnny

I wanted to show you something
but it's not there anymore.

Mangal

I think you are tired, kiddo. Go home and get some rest.

Johnny (confused)

OK, see you tomorrow

Johnny makes his way out and carries on, looking back at
the ring in the hope that Ali will be there and what he saw
wasn't a figment of his imagination.

28 INSIDE WARRIORS GYM. TRAINING (Week 2)
   28

Johnny makes his way into the gym. Mangal is in the
back, speaking to one of the guys who has been involved in a
fight outside of the gym. As Mangal is talking.

Man

Hey, boss, you better come out into the gym and see this.

Mangal

What is it?

Man

You have to come and see for yourself.

Mangal stops in mid-flow and makes his way out into the gym, where there is a crowd gathered. Mangal makes his way into the crowd, telling them to get out of the way, and as he gets to the front, not knowing what to expect. He is amazed to see what he is seeing. In front of him, he finds Johnny skipping rope like a professional. Everybody in the gym is shocked and amazed. They all start chanting, "Go, Johnny, go!"

Mangal

OK, everyone back to training.

Everyone goes back to their training

Mangal (laughs)

What did you have for breakfast?

Johnny

I need to tell you something.

Mangal

Let's do some training.

143

But?

Mangal
You can tell me later.

Johnny wants to tell Mangal about his encounter with Ali but doesn't know whether Mangal will believe him or think he has gone crazy. The gym empties out and it is apparent that Johnny has earned a newfound respect from his fellow training colleagues. Mangal can be heard faintly from the back room talking to the same man he was talking to earlier regarding his bad habits. Mangal was more of a social worker for the neighbourhood rather than a boxing teacher. Johnny sits on the edge of the boxing ring apron.

Ali (singing)
And darling stand
by me. When the night has
come and the land is dark
and the moon is the only
light we'll see. No I won't
be afraid. No Iiii won't be
afraid as long as you stand
by me.

Johnny
Moham, is that really you?

Ali
You ain't as dumb as you look, Kid.

Ali walks over to the bag and starts punching it. He then calls Johnny over and teaches him how to punch. Johnny starts to punch without getting tired. Johnny continues to punch and when he looks over his shoulder, he finds Mangal watching over him and not Ali.

Mangal
You are getting good. I
think those guys will have
their work cut out when it
comes to the tournament.

Johnny
I'm scared.

Mangal
Fear has its use but
cowardice has none.

Johnny
Do you believe in magic?

Mangal
Magic?

Johnny
Yes, magic.

Mangal
We all have some magic
inside of us, somewhere.

But it's down to you to
find it.

Johnny
I don't know how to explain it.

Mangal

Explain what?
Johnny
What I've been seeing.

Mangal
What have you been seeing?

Johnny
I don't know how to explain.

Mangal
You can try.

Johnny
I don't know how to…

Johnny is tearful and emotional. He takes off his gloves
and makes his way of the exit.

Mangal
He speaks to you, doesn't he?
Johnny stops in his tracks.

Mangal

Ali speaks to you, doesn't he?

Johnny

How do you know?

Mangal

He was singing to you earlier.
Wasn't he?

Johnny

Yes, he was. So you know
everything?

Mangal nods his head in agreement.

Johnny

Why didn't you say anything?

Mangal

I wanted you to figure it
out for yourself.

Johnny

Why?

Mangal

You would have thought
I had gone crazy.

Johnny
How long have you known?

Mangal
Long enough.

Johnny
What now?

Mangal
You let Ali teach you.

Johnny
Then what?

Mangal
Johnny kicks ass.

Johnny is relieved that Mangal knows everything and believes him.

Johnny
So you knew all along?

Mangal
Guilty.

Johnny
That's why you signed me up for this fight?

Mangal

You're getting good at this.

Mangal tells Johnny to go home and come back tomorrow ready to train hard as there is not long left now until the tournament.

Johnny

Why do I have to train hard
with Moham helping me?

Mangal

You can milk a cow the wrong way
once and still be a farmer, but
punch the wrong way in the boxing
ring once and you are in deep
trouble.

Johnny has found some extra confidence now and is ready for the challenge. Johnny makes his way home. Mangal makes his way to the window and sits on the bay, looking out into the street.

Mangal

Thanks, champ.

Ali

Everything god has created
has a purpose. The sun has
a purpose. The clouds have
a purpose. Rain has a purpose.
Trees have a purpose. Animals

have a purpose; even the
smallest insects and fish
in the sea have a purpose.
Regardless of how large or
how small, we were all born
to accomplish a certain task.
It is knowledge of that
purpose that enables every
soul to fulfil itself. One
person with knowledge of his
life's purpose is more powerful
that ten thousand working
without that knowledge.

<u>Mangal</u>
I guess I have found my purpose
by helping this kid.

There is a silence.

<u>Mangal</u>
Last time we spoke, you told me
you had a regret but never got
round to telling me what that was.

<u>Ali</u>
Turning my back on Malcolm
was one of the biggest
mistakes that I regret most
in my life. I wish I'd been
able to tell Malcolm I was

sorry, that he was right
about so many things. But
he was killed before I got
the chance. He was a
visionary; ahead of us all.
He was a great thinker and
an even greater friend. I
might never have become a
Muslim if it hadn't been
for Malcolm. If I could go
back and do it over again,
I would never have turned
my back on him.

All goes quiet once again.

Ali
When you saw me in the
boxing ring fighting,
it wasn't just so I could
beat my opponent. My
fighting had a purpose.
I had to be successful
in order to get people
to listen to the things
I had to say. I was
fighting to win the
world heavyweight title
so I could go out in
the streets and speak
my mind. I wanted to go

to the people, where
unemployment, drugs
and poverty were part of
everyday life. I wanted
to be a champion who
was accessible to everyone.
I hope to inspire others
to take control of their
lives and to live with
pride and self-determination.
I thought perhaps if
they saw that I was
living my life the way
I chose to live it, without
fear and with determination,
they might dare to take
risks that could set them free.

Mangal falls asleep whilst listening to Ali and when he wakes up, he finds Ali has gone.

29 <u>INSIDE WARRIORS GYM. TRAINING (Week 3)</u>
29

Through Mangal's diligence and Ali's help, Johnny has come a long way and is showing lots of improvement for the upcoming tournament. The news of his improvement has also passed to 'The Boss.'

<u>Johnny</u>
Which boxing video are you

showing me today?

Is it Friday today?

Johnny
Yes, it is.

Mangal
But you can speak to Ali
now, kiddo.

Johnny
A deal is a deal though.

Mangal
OK.

Johnny
So which video will it be?

Mangal
You'll find out later.

Johnny trains hard, harder than he has ever trained. After his training, Johnny helps with cleaning and closing up the gym.

Mangal
I'll finish up here, kiddo.
Just go and turn the

lights off in the changing
room.

Johnny goes and sits in the changing rooms where he falls asleep. Many hours have passed, and he suddenly wakes up. He can hear people talking and training in the gym. Johnny looks up at the clock in the changing room, which shows it has just passed mid-night. Johnny is surprised that there are people training in the gym at this time. Johnny peers around the corner of the changing room and sees Mangal sitting on the boxing ring apron with Ali talking and smiling. Mangal spots Johnny and shouts him over. As Johnny walks over, Ali and Mangal are in mid-conversation.

<u>Ali</u>

They write about how some
people took advantage of
me, stole from me and
how I let them get away
with it. Even when I knew
people were cheating me,
and how I let them get
away with it. Even when
I knew people were cheating
me, what was important was
how I behaved because I
have to answer to God.
I can't be responsible for
other people's actions:
They will have to answer
to God themselves.

Ali then spots Johnny and shouts whilst pointing to Johnny.

Ali

The champ is here.

Mangal

Where were you?

Before Johnny can respond, Ali takes Johnny by the hand.

Ali

Let me introduce you to some
of my friends.

Ali takes Johnny up to the heavy bag. A big man is punching into the bag as a small trainer holds onto the bag for his life. Each time the bag is punched, the trainer is lifted off his feet and the bag is left with a dent size of a watermelon.

Ali (to man punching the bag)

Hey, you big ugly bear.
Meet my friend, Johnny.

The man looks around with a mean look on his face.

Ali

Let's go meet some of the others.
Liston was the scariest guy I fought.

Johnny looks back to see that man who was punching the bag is Sonny Liston. Sonny Liston was one of the most menacing heavyweight boxing champions and died of a drug overdose in the 1970s.

Ali then walks Johnny over to a man practicing his technique on the speed bag

<u>Ali (whilst pointing)</u>

Now that there is the toughest
man I ever fought.

Ali points to Smokin' Joe Frazier.

<u>Ali</u>

He shook me in Manila.
We were gladiators. I
didn't ask no favours of
him and he didn't ask
none of me. I don't
like him, but I gotta
say, in the ring, he
was a man. In Manila,
I hit him punches;
those punches, they'd
have knocked a building
down. And he took 'em.
He took 'em, and he came
back, and I got to respect
that part of the man.
But I sent him home
worse than he came.

He was the one who spoke
about being nearly dead
in Manila, not me.
I heard somethin' once.
When somebody asked a
marathon runner what
goes through his mind
in the last mile or
two, he said that
you ask yourself,
'Why am I doin' this?'
You get so tired.
It takes so much
out of you mentally.
It changes you. It
makes you go a little
insane. I was thinkin'
that at the end.
Why am I doin' this?
What am I doin' in
here against this
beast of a man? It's
so painful. I must
be crazy. I always
bring out the best
in the men I fight,
but Joe Frazier, I'll
tell the world right
now, brings out the
best in me. I'm gonna
tell ya, that's one

helluva man, and
God bless him."

Frazier

If we were twins in the
belly of our mama. I'd reach
over and strangle him.

Ali

Joe Frazier is a good
man, and I couldn't
have done what I did
without him, and he
couldn't have done
what he did without
me. And if God ever
calls me to a holy
war, I want Joe
Frazier fighting
beside me.

Frazier

The butterfly and me
have been through some
ups and downs, and there
have been lots of
emotions, many of
them bad. But I have
forgiven him. I had
to. You cannot hold
out forever. There

were bruises in my
heart because of the
words he used. I
spent years dreaming
about him and wanting
to hurt him. But you
have got to throw
that stick out of
the window. Do not
forget that we needed
each other, to produce
some of the greatest
fights of all time.

Ali to Johnny.

Ali
I even wrote a poem for
This chump. Would you
like to hear it?

Johnny
Yeah. Of course.

Ali
Ali comes out to meet Frazier.
But Frazier starts to retreat.
If Frazier goes back any further,
he'll wind up in a ringside seat.
Ali swings to the left Ali swings to the right. Look at the kid
carry the fight.

Frazier keeps backing,
but there's not enough room. It's a matter of time
then Ali lowers the boom. Now, Ali lands to the right. What
a beautiful swing! And deposits Frazier
clean out of the ring.
Frazier's still rising.
But the referee wears a frown,
for he can't start counting
till Frazier comes down.
Now Frazier disappears from view.
The crowd is getting frantic, but our radar stations have
picked him up.
He's somewhere over the Atlantic.
Who would have thought that when they came to the fight,
that they would have witnessed the launching of a coloured
satellite!

Johnny is in awe of Ali telling these stories. Ali takes Johnny around the gym introducing him to all the greatest boxers in history Jack Johnson, Sugar Ray Robinson, Joe Louis, Rocky Marciano. Ali then comes and shakes hands with Mangal and says:

Ali
We'll be off now.

Mangal
See you next time, champ.

Ali (to Johnny)
Men often become what

160

they believe themselves to be. If I believe I cannot do something, it makes me incapable of doing it. But when I believe I can, then I acquire the ability to do it even if I didn't have it in the beginning. I believe in you. So does Mangal. We all do. So go out there and prove it to yourself.

Out of the corner of his eye, Johnny notices an Ali poster falling off the wall. He goes and puts it back; when he turns around, Ali and all the other boxing legends have gone.

Johnny
Where have they gone?

Mangal
It's getting late.

Johnny
Can you walk me home?

Mangal
Sure. Let me get my umbrella.

They both walk along the dark streets in the pouring rain, knowing that they are part of something magical. As they get to Johnny's place, his mum is waiting for him.

Mum
I've been worried sick
for you. Where have you
been?

Johnny
I was at the gym, Mum.
I told you I would be late.

Mum
I was still worried.

Mangal
I better get going.

Mum
Why don't you wait until
the storm calms down?

Mangal is waiting for the storm to calm down, and Johnny goes to sleep. Mum brings out some tea for Mangal.

Mum
Here take this. It's cold outside.

Mangal
Thanks.

Mangal is standing near the doorway drinking his tea.

Mum

I never got to say sorry to
you for the other day.

Mangal

How are you now?

Mum

I'm staying off the drugs.
It's not easy, but I'm trying.

Mangal

That's good. I better get going.

Mum

I wanted to say thank you for
everything you have done for
my son.

Mangal

He's a good kid.

Mum

In this day and age, no ones
got time to help anyone, so
why are you doing this?

Mangal

There were these two men who were
both seriously ill and in
the same hospital room. One

man was allowed to sit up in
his bed for an hour each
afternoon to help drain
the fluid from his lungs.
His bed was next to the
room's only window. The
other man had to spend all
his time flat on his back.
The men talked for hours on
end. They spoke of their
wives and families, their
homes, their jobs, their
involvement in the military
service, where they had
been on vacation.
Every afternoon when the
man in the bed by the window
could sit up, he would
pass the time by describing
to his roommate all the
things he could see
outside the window. The
man in the other bed
began to live for
those one-hour periods
where his world would
be broadened and
enlivened by all the
activity and colour
of the world outside.
The window overlooked

a park with a lovely
lake. Ducks and
swans played on the
water while children
sailed their model boats.
Young lovers walked arm
in arm amidst flowers
of every colour and
a fine view of the
city skyline could
be seen in the distance.
As the man by the window
described all this in
exquisite detail, the
man on the other side
of the room would
close his eyes and
imagine the picturesque
scene. One warm
afternoon the man by
the window described
a parade passing by.
Although the other
man couldn't hear the
band, he could see it.
In his mind's eye as
the man by the
window portrayed it
with descriptive
words. Days and weeks
passed. One morning,

the nurse arrived
to bring water for
their baths only
to find the lifeless
body of the man by
the window, who had
died peacefully in
his sleep.
She called the hospital
attendants to take the
body away. Later on,
the other man asked if
he could be moved next
to the window. The nurse
was happy to make
the switch, and
after making sure
he was comfortable,
she left him alone.
Slowly, painfully,
he propped himself
up on one elbow to
take his first
look at the real
world outside. He
turned to look out
the window beside
the bed. And you
know what?
It faced a blank wall.
The man asked the

nurse what could have
compelled his deceased
roommate who had
described such
wonderful things
outside this window.
The nurse responded
that the man was
blind and could not
even see the wall.
She said, "Perhaps
he just wanted to
encourage you." And
that man on that bed
over there.

30 THE DAY BEFORE THE TOURNAMENT. IN THE GYM 30

Johnny (to Mangal)
Aren't we training today?

Mangal
Not today, kiddo.

Johnny
Why not?

Mangal
I want to show you something.
Let's go.

Mangal takes his umbrella and locks the gym, as they make their way into a rickshaw (a three-wheel taxi).

Mangal(to taxi driver)
Downtown.

Johnny
Where are we going?

Mangal
You'll see.

31 THE DAY BEFORE THE TOURNAMENT.
DOWNTOWN 31

The rickshaw pulls up outside the venue where the tournament will take place. Mangal hands over the money to the driver as they both get out.

Johnny
Where are we?

Mangal
This is it, kiddo. This
is where you will be fighting tomorrow.

Both of them walk into the boxing arena, which used to be a cinema hall.

Johnny
This is huge.

Mangal nods his head in agreement.

Mangal
How are you feeling?

Johnny
Scared.

Mangal
Scared is good.

Johnny
Is it?

Mangal
Yes, everyone gets scared.

Johnny
Do you?

Mangal
All the time.

Johnny
What do you do when you
get scared?

Mangal
I talk to myself. What
about you?

Johnny
I eat.

Mangal
Oh. You must get very scared.

Johnny
Will you be here?

Mangal
Of course.

Johnny stands in the middle of the ring and looks up all around him, and as he looks into the audience, he can see all the boxing legends scattered around in different places. Johnny looks over at Mangal, and he smiles.

Mangal
Everything's going to
be alright, kiddo. Everything
is going to be OK.

Mangal and Johnny make their way back to the gym.

32 THE NIGHT BEFORE THE TOURNAMENT.
GYM 32

Mangal is sat on his rocking chair looking out of the huge windows as Johnny is sat looking through a book of Muhammad Ali pictures.

Sat by the window, the spirit of Ali appears.

Ali

There was this young boy
suffering from leukaemia,
Jimmy, who wanted to meet
me before my fight with
George Foreman in 1974.
Before the boy left, I had
a photograph taken with
Jimmy. I had that enlarged
and sent to the kid, with
the inscription: "You're going
to beat cancer. I'm going to
beat George. Love, Your friend,
Muhammad Ali." Two weeks later
Jimmy was in a hospital and
not expected to live. I was at
his bedside. When I walked in
he was lying in his bed, and I
saw that his skin was as white
as his sheets were.
Jimmy looked up at me with
bright eyes and called out:
"Muhammad, I knew you would come!"
I walked over to his bedside
and said, "Jimmy, remember what
I told you? I'm going to beat
George Foreman, and you're going
to beat cancer."
Jimmy looked
up at me and whispered: "No,
Muhammad. I'm going to meet

171

God and I'm going to tell him that you are my friend." The room was silent, and we were in tears.

I hugged Jimmy good-bye and
later that night, when we returned
to my training camp, none of us
spoke much A week later the boy
died. At his funeral, there had
been an open casket and that
the autographed picture was
beside Jimmy's head.
No matter what personal turmoil,
you will be going through right
now. It's down to you to put
that all out of your mind and
do the business.
The ultimate measure of a man
is not where he stands in moments
of comfort and convenience, but
where he stands at times of
challenge and controversy.

Then Ali disappears as the clock chimes midnight.

33 THE TOURNAMENT. THE DRAW 33

The draw of the tournament is scheduled for the morning of the tournament. The tournament consists of eight fighters, seven of which were from the boss camp. For one to become the champion, they would need to win three bouts. Each fight would be five rounds, with each round lasting two minutes.

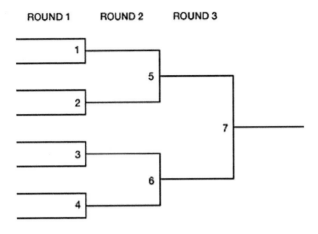

ROUND 1   ROUND 2   ROUND 3

1

5

2

7

3

6

4

Mangal, Johnny, Mum and Raju make their way to the tournament. As they walk into the hall, they spot the boss and his goons. Upon their arrival, Mangal learns that the draw has already been made. Johnny will be up against Shorty first. The nephew of the boss. The boss walks over to Mangal in an effort to intimidate him.

The Boss

So you actually showed up?

Mangal

Well, I wanted to be here,
when they got their asses
kicked.

Mangal said, pointing at Shorty, Slick and Big Brother. The boss laughs, as do his men.

The Boss
Good luck.

Mangal looks back at Johnny, who is looking rather scared.

Mangal
Don't worry. Let's go and get you ready

As Johnny walks away, he looks back towards Big Brother, who smiles. Johnny looks back at Raju, who says:

Raju
Smash his teeth out.

Johnny
I'll try.

34 THE TOURNAMENT. THE CHANGING ROOMS
   34

A small changing room with a locker, sink, toilet and bench is allocated to Johnny and Mangal. As they enter the room, Johnny looks around the room and opens his bag. Out of it, he takes out a poster of Ali which reads the caption: 'Float like a Butterfly' and sticks it on the door. Mangal warns Johnny not to eat or drink anything he is given but to only drink from the bottles of water Mangal has brought along as he is suspicious of foul play. Johnny is changed and sitting on the edge of the bench with Raju stood next to him as Mangal tapes up his hands before he puts the gloves on. Johnny is looking over at the poster of Ali. His mum is stood in the room praying for her son, hoping he doesn't get hurt.

Mangal

You're probably sitting
there thinking to yourself
right now, as I tape these
gloves up. Why am I doing
this? If you just sit there
pondering your confidence
starts to fade, it starts
to feel like you haven't
done any training, as if
you've forgotten what you
prepared to do. The changing
room is the worst part of
the fight game. Its where the
majority of the fights can
actually be won or lost. Your
mind will be playing all
sorts of tricks on you right
now but it's only natural. It's
how you deal with it that
matters. I want you to go out
there and float like a butterfly
and sting like a bee.

Mangal keeps on repeating this to psyche Johnny up, and then all of a sudden, there is a cold breeze and a chill down Johnny's spine. Johnny looks over to the doorway and sees spirit of Ali smile at him. Johnny springs up off the bench with a renewed vigour and does a quick succession of punches whilst repeating float like a butterfly, sting like a bee, float like a butterfly, sting like a bee.

35   THE TOURNAMENT. JOHNNY VS SHORTY 35

There is a knock at the door asking them to make their way into the ring. Mum kisses Johnny on the forehead and Raju gives Johnny a hug. Mangal leads Johnny out. As they make their way into the ring, they are being jeered and heckled. Johnny looks up and see's Ali dancing into the ring before him, so Johnny begins to imitate Ali. Johnny gets into the ring and slips and falls as everybody starts laughing. Mangal picks Johnny up off the floor.

Mangal
It's OK, kiddo. Focus,
focus, focus.

Shorty walks up to Johnny.

Shorty
You're dead.

Johnny
He looks angry.

Mangal
What were you expecting?
A peck on the cheek.

Both fighters make their way to the middle of the ring as the referee gives them instructions. They walk back to their corners.

Mangal

I'm proud of you, kiddo.

This is it. Float like a butterfly.

The bell rings; Shorty runs to the corner and starts hitting Johnny with a barrage of punches. One after the other, each punch hits Johnny in the face knocking him to the ground. The referee steps in, asking Shorty to go to his corner. Mangal is shouting at Johnny, telling him to get up. Johnny gets back to his feet as the fight continues. Shorty taunts Johnny over and over again whilst landing punch after punch on his face. Mangal watches from the corner with his head behind his hands. Johnny is momentarily distracted by the shouts that emanated from the rapidly growing crowd in the arena. Jeering is followed by cheers of abuse so loud that his attention is momentarily called away from the fight. Shorty's leg sweep out in a wide, graceful art, connecting with Johnny's ankles, throwing him off balance. Without even realizing what exactly is happening, Johnny finds himself flat on his back, sucking in deep breaths of air that seem devoid of oxygen. The subsequent tunnel vision that threatens to take away his sight clears with just enough time to roll away from a kick to the ribs. The bell rings for the end of the round. Johnny groggily walks back to the corner. Mangal shouts at the referee, reminding him this is a boxing match and not a kickboxing event.

Mangal

Are you OK, kiddo? It's
alright. You made it. Look,
you made it past the first
round. Now it's time for you
to throw some punches. Focus
focus, focus. Just keep your
hands up.

Round two, three and four are all one-sided, with Shorty landing many punches leaving Johnny bloody-nosed. The only thing Shorty hasn't done is knock Johnny out. He has done this intentionally under the orders of his uncle, who wants to make Johnny suffer for standing up to him and his family.

Mangal has his head next to Johnny as he sits on the stool in the corner at the end of Round four.

Mangal

Come on, kiddo. It's the
final round. You have to
do something. These are the
Last two minutes.

The bell rings for the 5th and final round. Johnny comes out with his hands up, protecting his swollen face. Shorty is gesturing to the crowd that this is the round he is going to knock Johnny out and taunting Johnny telling him to hit him with his best shot. Johnny staggered back when Shorty slammed his fist into his shoulder. He swung a roundhouse punch. Johnny bent backwards and felt his glove swish past his nose. Then all of a sudden, Johnny drops his left shoulder, winds up his right and throws an over-right cross that lands on the left jaw of Shorty, knocking him out cold. The crowd that was cheering and jeering is stunned into silence. The referee counts out Shorty 1–2–3–4–5–6–7–8–9–10. Mangal jumps into the ring and hugs Johnny.

Mangal

You did it, kiddo. You
did it.

The boss in the crowd is disgusted and is seen shouting and hurling abuse at everyone. Mangal accompanies Johnny back to the dressing room where his Mum and Raju are waiting.

Mangal (to Mum)

He's OK; he's OK. Don't worry.
He is going to be alright.

Johnny (to Mum)

I won!

Mum

I know. You were amazing

Raju hugs Johnny.

Mangal (to all)

I'll be back in a minute.

Mum and Raju cannot contain their happiness as Mangal leaves the dressing room and heads back to the ring to see who Johnny will be fighting next. He sees the other nephew of 'The boss', known as Slick, demolishing his opponent in the first round. The boss sees Mangal and walks over to him.

The Boss
Your boy got lucky.

Mangal
Lucky? He kicked your nephews
Behind.

There is a silence. Mangal turns to walk away but then turns back to the boss.

Mangal
Good luck.

Mangal makes his way back into the dressing room.

Mangal (to Johnny)
Make sure you drink plenty
of water.

Johnny
I won.

Mangal
I know. I was there.

Johnny

Oh, yeah!

Mangal

One down, two to go.

Raju (to Mangal)

Who will we be fighting

next?

Mangal avoids the question and asks Johnny to make sure
his laces are tied so he doesn't fall over.

Johnny

What's wrong?

Mangal

Nothing.

Then there's a knock at the door. Mangal looks at Johnny.

Mangal

Its time, kiddo.

Johnny

Already?

Mangal

Yep.

Johnny
Who am I fighting now?

Mangal
That doesn't matter.
What matters is that
you are going to go out
there and float like a
butterfly and sting like
a bee.

36 THE TOURNAMENT. JOHNNY VS SLICK 36

Mangal accompanies Johnny into the ring whilst Mum and Raju watch from the back of the hall. As they get closer to the ring. Many of the crowd have started cheering for Johnny. There seems to be a swing in popularity and less heckling. Johnny notices his opponent.

Johnny (to Mangal)
That's Slick.

Mangal
Oh, yeah!

Johnny
Oh, shit!

Mangal
It's time to get even, kiddo.
It's time to get even.

Johnny (to Mangal)
He's going to kick my ass.

Mangal
There's a solution for
that.

Johnny
What is it?

Mangal
You kick his first.

Johnny (sarcastically)
Wow. Why didn't I think
of that.

Mangal (whispers)
Float like a butterfly.

As Johnny steps into the ring, he feels a breeze and cold chill down his spine. He sees the spirit of Ali dancing around the ring, so he starts to imitate the shuffle and the dancing.

Slick to Johnny (shouting)
I'm going to drop you,
fat boy.

Johnny is unfazed and keeps his focus as the bell rings for the first round. Johnny meets Slick in the centre of the ring and hits him with a jab that catches Slick off guard. Johnny remains on his toes and throws a combination of punches, some catching his opponent whilst others grazing parts of his body. The bell rings for the end of the first round with Johnny on top. The second round begins and ends in the same fashion. In the background, the boss is seen whispering into the ear of Big Brother with some instructions. Big Brother makes his way to the ring, where he leans over the apron and whispers into the ear of Slick, who smirks. The referee looks over to 'The Boss', who nods his head. The bell then rings for the commencement of the bout and the beginning of round three. Both boxers come out, with Slick being the one with the more battered of the two. Johnny keeps him at a distance with his jab until Slick corners him off and grabs him pushing him into the corner and then grappling with him. Whilst getting up close, Slick lunges forward with his forehead smacking Johnny on the nose, causing blood to gush out, and then follows up with an elbow, hitting Johnny in the face as he falls to the ground. Mangal shouts out at the referee, who takes no action. It's quite evident that the referee has been bribed and paid off by 'The Boss.' There's a roar of protest from the crowd. Mangal urges Johnny to get to his feet as the referee starts counting. Johnny staggers back to his feet at the count of eight to the amazement of Slick, who is looking at Big Brother, not knowing how Johnny managed to survive. The bell then rings for the end of the round. Johnny makes his way to the corner, not knowing where he is.

Mangal

Are you OK, kiddo?

Mangal touches Johnny's nose, making Johnny scream in agony. From his experience, Mangal knows that the nose is broken but plays it down.

Mangal

It's not as bad as it

Feels, kiddo.

Mangal cleans up all the blood from Johnny's face and tells him he's going to stop the fight.

Johnny (to Mangal)

No please don't stop the

fight.

Mangal

You have got nothing to

prove anymore, kiddo.

Johnny (to Mangal)

I can beat him. Just tell

me what I need to do.

Please.

Mangal

OK, kiddo, you let him get

up close again. As he comes

on the inside, he will try to

lunge at you with his head

and I want you to step to

the side and hit him in the

face with your elbow and then
carry on punching him.

Johnny nods his head.

Mangal
Protect your nose, kiddo.

The bell rings for the fourth round. Johnny retreats back
into the corner cautiously and allows Slick to come towards
him. Whilst on the back foot Johnny allows his opponent to
get close up, and just as he is about to jump forward with his
head, Johnny steps out of the way and swings his elbow into
the jaw of Slick, snapping his head back in bewilderment and
causing him to fall to the ground like a sack of potatoes. The
referee is shocked by the events that have transpired before
his very own eyes, causing a delay in him starting the count.
Members of the crowd start to shout, "Fix, Fix, Fix," forcing
the referee to begin his count. Slick tries to get back to his
feet, only to fall through the ropes and out of the ring. Mangal
jumps into the ring with the biggest smile on his face. Mum
and Raju can be seen hugging and screaming with joy in the
background. All the boxing legends (Sonny Liston, Joe
Frazier, Sugar Ray Robinson, Rocky Marciano, Floyd
Patterson, Henry Cooper) are standing ringside high fiving
each other. Ali jumps into the ring and does the Ali shuffle.

Ali (shouting)
I told you he would do
it. I told you. All you
suckers bow. I told you.

Mangal is holding Johnny to make sure he is alright. They both look over at Ali and smile.

Ali starts singing the song 'I wish it would rain' by The Temptations. As the song becomes part of the background music, Johnny is helped out of the ring and to the dressing room. On the way back, many people are cheering, shaking his hand, congratulating both him and Mangal, and tapping Johnny on the head. The Boss is angry and disgusted as both Johnny and Mangal walk past him. As they get to the dressing room and Mangal closes the door, the music stops. Mum comes and gives Johnny a big hug, as does Raju. Both are elated and happy and at the same time concerned and worried with all the marks and blood on Johnny's face. Then all goes quiet as footsteps can be heard outside, getting closer to the door, and then all of a sudden, there is a knock at the door. Raju goes over to open the door; as soon as he opens the door, he is thrown aside by a man. Raju falls, banging his head against a locker. Mum runs over to help him as Johnny looks over with concern. The boss walks in whilst facing up to Mangal, giving him the stare with an angry look on his face, pointing his finger at Mangal.

The Boss
You better not even think
about winning the next fight?

Mangal
Are you scared?

There is no response from the boss and a silence.

Mangal
You are actually scared,
aren't you?

The Boss
You are testing my patience,
old man.

Mangal stands up next to the boss right in his face staring at him.

Mangal
I'm not scared of you. Do
whatever you want. We
are going to come out to
ring and not only that; my
boy is going to win and
there's nothing you can do
to stop him.

The boss turns to his nephew, 'Big Brother'.

The Boss
I want you to make him suffer.

Big Brother
Oh, I sure will.
(whilst spitting on Johnny's Face)

The boss is still up close to Mangal.

The Boss
Don't say I didn't warn you
Both.

Mangal
God help us.

The boss and Big Brother leave the room angrily with their entourage. Mangal walks over and closes the door. He walks over to a tape recorder in the corner of the room and presses the play button. The song called 'Peace Train' by Cat Stevens begins to play as Mangal walks over to Johnny.

Mangal
I'll be happy with whatever
you decide, kiddo.

Johnny
What would Mohamm do?

There is a silence as Mangal looks over at the poster of Ali on the wall. Johnny also looks over at the poster. Both Mangal and Johnny then look at each other. Johnny springs up off the bench.

Johnny
I know what Mohamm would do?

Both Mangal and Johnny smile and shout: "Float like a Butterfly."

Johnny walks towards the ring with all the spirits of the boxing legends on either side of him, led by Ali. Johnny staggers to the ring with a smile on his face. Mangal takes the stool and tells Johnny to sit down and get some rest as Big Brother enters the ring. The lights go out and there is silence. As the lights return, Big Brother appears standing, holding his hands up in victory as a man follows, holding his championship belt. He walks down the aisle towards the ring with the crowd still in complete silence. He steps into the ring, walks over to Johnny and kicks the stool he is sitting on, making him fall to the ground. A huge roar is heard from the crowd, who are ready for this fiery contest. Mangal helps Johnny up to his feet.

Big Brother goes to his corner wearing his loose-fitting black shorts with 'BOSS' written on the front. He bends down and stretches his back. He turns his head from left to right, popping it with a series of clicks in rapid succession. Then he proceeds to do the same with the rest of his body as he loosens up the rest of his body. Both fighters make their way to the centre of the ring as Big Brother looks down on Johnny using his height advantage. They take the instructions from the referee as Big Brother looks down at Johnny and says, "Get ready to go to the hospital."

Johnny turns back, having his gum shield put in. Both Mangal and Johnny put their heads together with the spirit of Ali also in the huddle. "Float like a butterfly, float like a butterfly."

Big Brother begins the first round by attacking Johnny with unconventional and provocative right arm swings followed by the elbow. This aggressive tactic puts Johnny on the back foot and Big Brother hits him solidly a number of times.

Johnny begins to lean on the ropes and cover-up, letting Big Brother punch him on the arms and body. Big Brother uses his height advantage to lean on Johnny and catch him with blows to the back of the head with no reprimand from the referee. Johnny remains on the ropes taking every opportunity to shoot straight right punches to Big Brother's face. Big Brother's swagger from the opening bell is mesmeric, showing he is the better fighter of the two. He is snapping back the head of his foe with left-right combinations before rocking him against the ropes. Johnny, with his extra weight, appears a yard off the pace and there for the taking. The bell goes for the end of the round. Johnny struggles back to the corner and slumps on the stool with a sigh of relief, having survived that round.

Mangal
You OK, kiddo? You need
to keep that nose covered.

Johnny (to Mangal)
I can't beat him. He's too
good. I can't beat—

Mangal (interrupts)
Oi. Oi. Don't you quit on

me now. Don't you think Ali
was scared when he fought
Liston? Don't you think Ali
was scared when he fought
Frazier? Don't you think he
was scared when he fought
Foreman? Of course, he was.
It's OK to be scared. But
you're better than him.

Mangal points over at Big Brother in the opposite corner.

<u>Mangal</u>
Look at him. Go on, look
at him. You've just beaten
up two of his friends. Don't
let him tell you what you
can and can't do. So let's
get it together and do this.
This one's for Ali.

<u>Johnny</u>
This one's for Ali?

<u>Mangal (nodding his head)</u>
Yep. This one's for Ali.

Johnny seems to have got some confidence back in him.

<u>Johnny</u>
This one's for Ali?

Mangal (nodding his head)
Yep. This one's for Ali.

Mangal
You can do this, kiddo.

Johnny
Float like a butterfly.

Mangal
Float like a butterfly.

Having pressured the champion in the second, Big Brother pounds away at Johnny's body, making him eat a series of combinations for his troubles in the third before being knocked down twice in quick succession. The referee allows the fight to continue so the champion can dish out more punishment to the challenger. The champion is plucking the wings off the butterfly. In a rare show of abandon—the pair swung for the rafters for a 20-second period that almost brings the arena to its foundations. Big Brother is pouncing and toying with angles, while Johnny acts as the human version of sinking sand, continuously attempting to drag his opponent into trench warfare. By the end of the fourth it's quite clear that Johnny hasn't got any more to give. Johnny is in the corner sat on his stool, breathing heavily for air.

Mangal
You can do this, kiddo.
One more round.

Johnny

I'm tired.

Mangal

I know, kiddo.

Then the spirit of Ali enters the rings, comes over to Johnny and passes through him, sending a chill down this spine. All of a sudden, there is a burst of energy, and Johnny springs up as Mangal places the gumshield in his mouth; they both smile, acknowledging each other.

The bell rings as both fighters meet in the centre of the ring. Johnny is moving away from the ever-pursuing champion, hands at his side, reminiscent of Ali. Big Brother throws a left at the ever-retreating challenger, but by the time he got there, Johnny was gone. He returned scant seconds later to throw a flurry of punches off his left jab. Encouraged by his success, Johnny shoots left to the body followed by three lefts to the head. Big Brother seemed paralyzed and unable to find his elusive tormentor, steadfastly standing like a tree while Johnny floats around him, picking his spots. Finally, Big Brother gets going first, cutting the ring off on Johnny and landing a stiff left to the head. It was a mistake, as Johnny moved out of harm's way, and on his way threw a flurry of six punches, all landing to Big Brother's guarded but still unprotected head. Unable to find any gear but straight ahead, came in again, and for his trouble, received a volley of eight more shots to the head, all landing. A trickle of blood could be seen on Big Brother Johnny begins to play the role of a finger painter, smearing it across the whole of his face with a jab, a straight right, a hook and a right. Johnny skips around

194

the ring as his opponent wearily trudges. Once more, the champion tries to go the only way he had ever learned to go—forward—and, for his efforts, he is caught with more punches, this time a left and a right. He stood in the middle of the ring like a puppet that had his strings cut

Johnny then hears Ali whisper: "The shuffle kiddo, the shuffle." And then it happened. Preceded by an accentuated five-step in-place tango manoeuvre he called 'the Ali Shuffle', Johnny threw a left and then a right reminiscent of the one Ali had caught the incoming Sonny Liston with at Lewiston, Maine in 1965. Big Brother hung in mid-air momentarily and then fell sprawling to the canvas. Big Brother unable to get up and make an attempt to defend himself as blood pours down from his nose is down and out. Johnny cannot believe his eyes. He has beaten his nemesis. He has done the unthinkable. He has done what no one thinks he could do. Just like Ali when he beat George Foreman in 1974, Kinshasa, Zaire. Everyone in the arena is on their feet, cheering and applauding. Mum and Raju run into the ring whilst hugging Johnny and Mangal.

The boss comes over to Mangal and finally accepts the better man won and tells Big Brother to present the championship belt to Johnny.

38 THE FAREWELL 38

Mangal, Johnny, Mum and Raju make their way outside from the arena, and they are still being congratulated. A rickshaw is waiting. Mangal asks Mum and Raju to get in and tells Mum that he and Johnny will be home in a short while. Raju hugs Johnny whilst getting into the rickshaw, and Mum does the same. She then pops out of the rickshaw and hugs Mangal thanking him for everything with tears in her eyes. She sits in the rickshaw, and they all wave as the rickshaw disappears into the distance.

Mangal and Johnny start walking down the street into the sunset.

Mangal

How are you feeling, kiddo?

Johnny

Hungry.

Mangal

Me too.

Both of them smile as the song 'Don't worry, be happy' by Bobby McFerrin plays. Then as they walk further down, the spirit of Ali appears in the middle as both Mangal and Johnny walk on either side doing a celebration dance.

The End